**Gabi clenched her fi
watched Nate stare a
with something like**

Was it that easy for him? To come in here after all this time and just be a father? Gabi hated the twist of resentment and tried to turn away.

"Which..." Nate swallowed visibly. "Which..."

Anger turned to pity in an instant. "Ana is on the left. She sleeps like the dead. Her hair is just a little shade lighter than Antonio's, though you'd not be able to see it now. Antonio, he's the light sleeper. He'll wake up if a pin drops," she said around a smile, her whisper dropping to an even quieter level, in case she conjured him from his sleep. "Ana is stubborn and determined. Antonio is happy and easygoing, but..."

"But?" Nate turned, his head close to hers, closer than she'd realized.

"But a little more delicate," she said.

Nate nodded, the darkness of the room preventing her from seeing how he had interpreted her descriptions of their children. *Their* children.

Pippa Roscoe lives in Norfolk near her family and makes daily promises to herself that this is the day she'll leave the computer to take a long walk in the countryside. She can't remember a time when she wasn't dreaming about handsome heroes and innocent heroines. Totally her mother's fault, of course—she gave Pippa her first romance to read at the age of seven! She is inconceivably happy that she gets to share those daydreams with you all. Follow her on Twitter @pipparoscoe.

Books by Pippa Roscoe

Harlequin Presents

The Wife the Spaniard Never Forgot
His Jet-Set Nights with the Innocent
In Bed with Her Billionaire Bodyguard

A Billion-Dollar Revenge

Expecting Her Enemy's Heir

The Royals of Svardia

Snowbound with His Forbidden Princess
Stolen from Her Royal Wedding
Claimed to Save His Crown

Visit the Author Profile page
at Harlequin.com for more titles.

Twin Consequences of That Night

PIPPA ROSCOE

HARLEQUIN

PRESENTS

ISBN-13: 978-1-335-59337-5

Twin Consequences of That Night

Recycling programs for this product may not exist in your area.

Harlequin Enterprises ULC
22 Adelaide St. West, 41st Floor
Toronto, Ontario M5H 4E3, Canada
www.Harlequin.com

Printed in Lithuania

MIX
Paper | Supporting responsible forestry
FSC® C021394

Twin Consequences
of That Night

For my incredible niece Izzi,

You are such an inspiration, and it has been nothing but a joy to watch you become the woman you are today.

Your strength, conviction, sense of adventure and sense of humour are boundless and wonderful, and I'm lucky to be part of your life.

All my love, always,

Auntie Pippa

xx

CHAPTER ONE

Nate was in his sister's flat. It looked the same, but certainly didn't feel the same. There was a glass of wine in his hand, but he couldn't remember how it had got there, and nor could he smell the rich fruity scent of what he was sure would be a Beaujolais. His vision was fuzzy at the edges and his sister was saying something, but he couldn't hear it. Sound was muffled, as if his head was wrapped in a blanket. His vision was tunnelled and her eyes widened in alarm, her mouth opening in shock, just as he was drowned in blackness...

'Mr Harcourt, can you hear me? Mr Harcourt?'

He was being shaken roughly, pain slicing into his head. Something was wrong. His sister was sobbing. Begging.

'Please help him. Please do something.'

His body rolled viciously and he landed on a bed with a thud. A light shone in his eye, blinding him, but he couldn't close it. He tried to smack the hand away, but his arm wouldn't move.

'His left pupil's blown.'

Words like 'CT', 'angiogram', 'bloods' swam as he tried to find his sister, but he couldn't move a muscle.

He was in hell, his body on fire. He felt everything: each needle-stick, each poke and prod, the knuckle against the arch of his foot. But his body wasn't reacting. Nothing.

Numb, but not numb.

'What's going on?'

Hope sounded so scared that it terrified him. He knew that fear, the incomprehensible touch of death come to steal away loved ones, and he wouldn't inflict that on her. He couldn't.

The high-pitched moan of the monitor screamed until it descended into irregular pips.

'You're going to be fine, Nate. I promise. The best doctor is flying in right now to do the operation.'

What operation? What had happened?

'Nate, you're going to be fine,' his sister whispered into his ear. 'I promise.'

The cabin door on his small private jet slammed shut, yanking him from the nightmare that wasn't a nightmare. Nightmares were baseless fears: terrors of the unknown, irrational monsters dredged from the unconscious. What Nate had just experienced was a sleeping memory. Events that had been real and had happened more than two years ago, the night he'd returned from the disaster that was the Casas deal. The night a headache that had started in Madrid had ended with him collapsed on the floor of his sister's London apartment.

Of course, it had never crossed anyone's mind to announce to the world that Nathanial Harcourt, English billionaire, had suffered a cerebral aneurism. It hadn't

even required discussion. It was imperative not only for
Harcourts, but also the three businesses that he owned
personally, that news of such a weakness not threaten
the financial bottom line.

It had been somewhat bitterly amusing to Nate that
the idea that he was taking a self-indulgent journey of
discovery in Goa was favourable to a near death experience to his board members and the public. So it had
been kept secret because of vultures, economics and
public perception.

All of it: the successful operation done in London that
very night, the medical flight to the private Swiss hospital where he would not only receive round-the-clock
medical attention, but also intense and expert rehabilitation until he could return with absolutely no evidence
of any mental or physical incapacity.

Only his sister and his grandfather knew that instead
of sunning himself on a beach he'd been learning how
to *make pain his friend'*.

Bugger that.

The initial operation had been a walk in the park
compared to the long-term fallout. He might have been
in the best private medical facility that money could
buy, but it didn't mean a thing. The rehab, the fatigue,
the headaches, the clicks he heard whenever he moved,
the hearing loss, the jaw pain, the back pain, the slowed
reaction times? These were untenable to a man who had
been raised to see weakness as anathema, an abomi-
nation to be rooted out, cut out like a cancer before it
could impact stock share prices and public perception.

They were daily reminders, taunts, cruel and constant, in those first twenty months, reminding him that he was not the man he'd once been. That he needed to be careful, watchful of his health, his diet, his exercise… his stress levels. For a man who'd rarely denied himself a thing, his life had become about strictures and rules: scheduled medications and vitamins, check-ups booked in the diary years in advance.

And his grandfather refusing to meet his eye.

'You should consider reducing your workload. Considerably.'

For more than two years, Nate had worked harder than he ever had before to get back to where he could resume his life seamlessly, so that he *didn't* have to reduce his workload 'considerably'. He had grown his hair out a little—attributing it to his self-indulgent adult 'gap years' and not down to the fact that it now hid a scar line. He had lost weight which, according to the latest headlines, was from partying too hard rather than a loss of appetite from diminished aptitude for taste and smell.

But the impact on reactions, his decisiveness, the things that had made him a truly excellent businessman? Utterly devastating. It was as if he were constantly wading through liquid amber: holding him back, slowing him down, making it hard to think and breathe sometimes.

He saw it in the faces of his staff, his sister, his grandfather. The confusion, the doubt, the frustration with his slowness… He just wasn't the same as he'd been before. The doctors insisted that it wasn't *'a cause for concern'*. That it would *'go away with time'*. And he could see it; they just didn't understand. Didn't get what it was like to have your whole life change with the flip of a switch. A switch that had flipped the moment he'd returned from that damn business with the Casases.

'Flight time to Madrid is just over two hours from London, Mr Harcourt.'

Nate nodded to acknowledge he'd heard the air stewardess making her way towards him. He closed his eyes, hoping to relieve the ache left by the nightmare that wasn't a nightmare, and leaned back against the headrest.

'And if there's anything,' she continued, 'at all,' she said, pressing a hand on his shoulder, his eyes opening quickly enough to see a flash of fire engine red talon against his white shirt, 'I'd be very happy to oblige.'

If there had been any doubt about the intent of her words, it was obliterated by the lascivious look in her eyes.

A little over two years ago Nathanial Harcourt would have smirked, caught her wrist, pulled her into his lap and given her, in vivid Technicolor, her heart's desire, uncaring of what the captain and his co-pilot did or didn't see.

Back then, he'd been in his prime, the *enfant terrible* of the British business scene. He owned three companies personally and was the CFO of his family's business, Harcourts—a brand and name synonymous with luxury, exclusivity and opulence. The international department store had been in his family for generations, and he was hotly tipped to be the next CEO. After all, he'd been groomed to lead it, first by his father and then, after his parents' death, by his grandfather. But in order to prove himself to the board, he'd been on his way to Madrid to secure a deal with a Spanish fashion conglomerate, Casas Fashion. And success had been within his reach...

Until he'd met Gabriella Casas.

Nate looked down to find his hand fisted on his thigh and the air stewardess still waiting for him to respond to her invitation.

'Thank you, darling, I'll take a whisky,' he said, purposely misunderstanding her, his voice full of a gravel dragged from bitterness the air stewardess was utterly oblivious to.

She withdrew her hand from his shoulder and, masking her disappointment, disappeared towards the jet's impressive galley.

Nate looked out of the small round window, seeing the moon painting clouds in an unearthly glow.

Gabriella Casas.

Even now his body betrayed him, reacting to the memory of her in ways that he couldn't control. Erotic tension teased him into an arousal he didn't want. His stomach clenched as the small private jet taking him back to Madrid hit an air pocket and dropped him back into the first time he'd laid eyes on her, when he'd not known her name. When he'd arrogantly thought it wasn't even important.

She was, simply put, the most beautiful woman he'd ever seen. And Nathanial Harcourt, who *never* made the first move, had been completely unable to stop himself. Large, startlingly hazel eyes locked on his and he felt as if he'd been punched in the solar plexus. He'd spent years thinking over every single moment of that night, unpicking where he'd gone wrong, where he'd failed to spot the warning signs. Wondering if the cerebral aneurism had perhaps already started affecting him even then.

'Would you like a drink?'

'I don't want you to get the wrong idea.'

'I only asked you for a drink—nothing more.'

Nate could still feel the heat of her gaze on him, seemingly as unable to look away as he'd been. He, who had seduced countless women in countless countries, had been utterly seduced by what he thought was an innocent.

'I want to talk to you.'

'And I want to hear everything you want to say, but first... I need... I want to do...this.'

He hadn't been able to stop himself. He should have asked first, but the sheer shared desire he could feel between them made the air so thick with want it was almost impossible to think. A kiss…just a touch of lips, that was all he'd intended. But he hadn't realised, hadn't known that he'd not be able to stop at that. And even then, he'd wondered whether he'd be able to spend the rest of his life without her in it. It was like heaven, just before it turned into hell.

The next morning he'd opened his eyes to an empty bed and he'd been shocked. A cynical part of himself now mocked the irony mercilessly. The number of beds he'd sneaked away from hardly stacking up to the single time it was done to him. He'd sat up, looking around at his clothes strewn about the floor, each one a sensual memory and a censure at the same time.

He'd caught sight of a small glittery clutch beneath the side table and reached for it. With no compunction whatsoever, he'd opened it, looking for some sign of who he had spent the most spectacular night of his life with. No phone, no ID, just a credit card and a room key: *G Casas*.

He'd stared at it numbly for moments while his usually rapid-fire brain made sluggish connections it didn't want to make. Anger poured through his veins and he dressed with furious, jerky movements.

After he'd realised who he had spent the night with, he'd paid his investigators more than triple their rate to find out whatever it was that had been missed the first time, because he'd known that they must have missed something. That was when he'd discovered the depths of Renata Casas's treachery.

Gabriella Casas had been, he could only presume, sent by her mother to seduce him, probably because her own stomach-churning attempts to do so had failed spectacularly. He should have paid heed to the gleam in Renata Casas's eye as he'd informed her they would be keeping things strictly professional. But he hadn't expected her to send her own daughter to distract him from the fact that they were trying to fleece him out of millions by selling him shares in a company they didn't own.

But confronting Renata and Gabriella Casas that afternoon had been a mistake. That was the conclusion he'd come to after reliving the events of that twenty-four-hour period over and over again through the merciless sessions of physio and rehab.

'Get her out of here. I never want to look at her ever again. She's no better than a whore.'

Gabriella's mother's words stung like a vicious slap. And he'd hardened himself against the image of Gabriella standing there shaking, her eyes full of pleas, regrets, apologies.

Lies, it was all lies.

Renata had illegally tried to sell him shares she didn't own in a business that wasn't hers. Her *son's* business.

'Lady, you're crazy. My lawyers are going to go through everything with a fine-tooth comb and when they're done...'

He'd left them with that threat and returned straight to his sister's apartment in London. And then a small blood vessel had ruptured everything he'd ever known.

Nate knew that it was irrational to link the two together—emotional rather than evidentiary. But he kept telling himself that once he was done with Casas Textiles, his whole life would get back to normal. Just like it was before.

Which was why, two years later, he was flying to Spain to be a key witness in a fraud and embezzlement trial against Renata Casas. Nathanial Harcourt never made a promise he didn't keep and now he was here to make good on it.

Renata Casas and her daughter would rue the day they'd tried to make a fool out of Nate Harcourt.

'Are you okay in there?' Gabi's brother worriedly called through the toilet door. Javier Casas was worried about the idea of her giving evidence at her mother's trial, but that wasn't why she was hiding in the bathroom.

'Yes, just a minute,' she replied.

She stared at herself in the mirror. The long dark tresses that she had once taken so much pride in were now pulled back in a chaotic bun—not artfully designed by a stylist, but thrown back with little time or care. Clothes that had once been so much of her focus—fabric, colour, style, cut, *design*—were now chosen by cleanliness level and, even then, the top she wore betrayed a spatter of tomato sauce from lunch. Cheeks that had once been flushed pink with youth and excitement were now thinner, cheekbones pronounced from lack of opportunity rather than diet or contour. She looked pale, putting it kindly, she thought as she skirted over the thumbprints of darkness smudged beneath her eyes.

She'd spent too long staring at the newspaper she'd sneaked in here with her. The words had long ago become blurred and the only thing she could see clearly was the eyes of the still handsome man she had spent one spectacular night with, a little over two years ago. The picture was black and white, but she would have sworn she could see the espresso-rich depths of his gaze, staring straight at the camera—staring straight at her.

Nathanial Harcourt.

He'd grown his wheat blond hair out. That night, it had been short, efficient. She remembered the feel of his scalp beneath her nails, the way he'd unfurled beneath her as she'd done that while they'd kissed. Her breath caught as she remembered the feel of his tongue, his touch, his need for her. The way his skin had pebbled as she chased the goosebumps with her kisses, fascinated by his reaction to her all the while he was trying to distract her with her own responses. She blinked back tears, remembering how they'd laughed, how he'd let her get things wrong. He'd let her explore him, learn the feel of things, of them together, the way her heart pounded, passion sighed, her legs trembled, her hands fisted, the way she had gasped, the way he had growled. The way that—

No!

She swiped at a tear with one hand as the other curled the paper beneath her fingers, clenched and furious.

No. She'd tried to reach him every day for nearly two years.

Every. Day.

Emails. Phone calls. If she'd had a fax number, she would have tried that too. At one point she'd been half convinced that there was a conspiracy, that people were actively trying to keep her away from him. She'd tried everything she could think of, bar getting on a flight, and the only reason she hadn't done that was that she simply hadn't been physically able to. She'd reached out to contacts in the fashion industry, anything to get a message to the CFO of Harcourts department store. She'd even gone to the Spanish flagship store in Madrid and they'd eventually called security. And the shame! The shame at abasing herself like that had laid fresh hurt over old scars in her battered self-confidence. And all that time he'd been sunning himself on a beach in South Asia.

But now he was here. In Madrid. Having been called

as a witness in the trial of the century, if the gossip rags were to be believed.

No one had thought that Nathanial Harcourt would actually do it, least of all her mother. But apparently the last thing he had done before disappearing on his extended 'sabbatical' was file charges against Renata for what she had done.

Gabi hadn't been surprised though. She'd realised what would happen the night she'd met him—the fateful night that had changed the entire course of her life. And no, she could never bring herself to regret it, not for a second. But so much had happened because of it.

That night, her mother had sent Gabi to Nate with every intention of having her daughter seduce the rich English businessman in order to distract him from her illegal wrongdoings. Instead, for Gabi it had been the final straw. She had gone there to tell Nathanial Harcourt that her mother didn't have the ability or permission to sell shares in her son's company and that he should leave without looking back.

She'd wanted to tell him, but she'd been so stunned by him, by his apparent interest in her, she'd been struck silent. She tried, several times, but it was as if she couldn't say it and he wouldn't hear it. His flirtation had undone her, and her innocent responses had strangely delighted him, and for just one night she'd thought she'd found someone who had seen her, understood what was at the core of her. Otherwise, she never would have done what she did.

But when he'd tracked her down at her mother's house the next day, after she'd fled the hotel, the betrayal she'd seen in his eyes before the mask came down was the first of many blows her heart would receive that day.

'You send her after me like some Mata Hari and now you want to get rid of her?'

'Why would I want her? She's no better than a whore.'

The vicious shock of her mother's accusation had struck another blow. And when Nate had refused to even look at her, defend her, argue that what they'd shared had been more, it had scattered those broken pieces to the four winds.

'Sweetheart, are you okay?' Emily whispered, gently knocking against the bathroom door. Her sister-in-law's concern finally nudged at her conscience. Gabi shook off her thoughts, gave herself a stern *pull yourself together* glare in the mirror and opened the door into a familiar, loving, chaotic mess.

'Mamá! Mamá! Mamá!'

The sound of little feet running down the long hallway towards her lifted her heart at the same time as bringing a damp heat to her eyes. Her babies, Ana and Antonio, with matching grins, pink cheeks and dark mahogany gazes, raced towards her on feet only just becoming steady.

She crouched down to meet them and took them both in her arms, and after letting the moment soothe the ache in her heart, she reached to tickle them both until they all descended into giggles. She bent her head to their crowns and inhaled the sweet smell of her children and then gently pulled back.

'What mischief are you two up to then?' she demanded.

'They understand that? In English?' Javier asked

in Spanish, leaning against the doorframe, wiping his hands from washing up after lunch.

'They know that while we're here we speak English,' Gabi replied in English.

Emily slipped beneath her husband's arm, carrying her own daughter, Lily, a pretty curly-haired one-year-old, and for a second Gabi's heart ached. She breathed past the hurt of the sight of her brother with his arm around his wife and child. It was the family unit that she'd always wanted but had never had, not only for herself but for her children.

'I'm fluent now in Spanish if it's easier?' Emily offered.

Gabi smiled and stuck to the lie that she wanted Ana and Antonio to be bilingual for their sake. Javi, her brother, had never pushed Gabi to tell him the name of the twins' father. She was sure that he had figured it out, but he'd never said anything. Their relationship, so much better since she had left her mother's, had involved a lot of support and a lot of work, and so much of it was built on trust. Trust that when she needed to she'd tell him. Trust that he would be there when she did.

Her brother had given Gabi absolutely everything—he'd needed to, because when she'd left Renata's house she'd left with nothing but what she'd been wearing. She'd not gone back since the night of the argument between Nate and Renata. There was not a single thing in that house she'd wanted. And while Javi wouldn't have it any other way, there was a huge part of Gabi that wished she could find some way of being independent.

'*Cara, you have twins. They should be your focus,*

not worrying about money or housing. Especially not when I can give those things to you.'

She knew that what her brother had said made sense. She would *never* deprive her children of any kind of shelter or support just because of her own stubborn desire to provide for her family herself. But still…it cut her deep.

It hadn't been easy—discovering she was pregnant just when she had lost everything she had known. Realising that the father of her children wanted absolutely nothing to do with her. Becoming a mother at the age of twenty-three and losing what few friends she did have to partying and clubbing and travels around the world. Watching the hopes and dreams she'd had for her fashion designs slip through her fingers had closed something off within her.

But no matter what imaginary future she'd once dreamed of, the moment that she'd held both her babies in her arms, she knew—*knew*—that she'd never have had it any other way. She would protect these two innocent children with every single fibre of her being. She would love them so much that it would make up for any lack of father figure. These two children would not have the same upbringing that she had. No matter what she had to do to make that happen.

'Is it the court case?' Javi asked, the concern etched across his features in frown lines. 'You don't have to be a witness for the prosecution, you know. They've got enough evidence and even if they didn't—'

'It's fine,' Gabi dismissed, easing herself up from the floor and watching her twins run off into the sitting room of Javi's apartment in Madrid. 'It's the right thing to do,' she said with a simple shrug. And it really was. She wouldn't shy away from the horrible truths about her mother. 'I'm just sorry it meant uprooting everyone from Frigiliana to come here.'

Emily shushed her with a wave. 'I've been wanting to come back into town for ages.'

Gabi smiled at Emily's use of 'town' for Spain's capital city. Her Spanish was almost perfect now, but the Britishisms she used still identified her as a foreigner. Emily, who had been estranged from her brother for five years at one point, was now almost as close as a sister. But there were still some things that Gabi needed to keep to herself. And one of those things was Nathanial Harcourt.

The same Nathanial Harcourt who was due to give evidence. The prosecutor had assured her that they wouldn't meet as they were scheduled at different times for the day. He'd explained that the delays court cases often experienced meant that it was highly likely she'd be pushed back to the next day anyway.

But Gabi wasn't so sure. She couldn't shake the feeling that, having put him firmly from her mind and life when the twins turned one, a reckoning was upon her, one way or another.

CHAPTER TWO

NATE PEERED UP at the courthouse as he walked towards the entrance. He paused at the top of the steps, taking a breath, buttoning his blazer and smoothing down his tie. He was finally ready to put this whole entire mess behind him. He'd leave here after giving testimony against Renata and her attempt to defraud him and steal money from him, and then liquidate his remaining shares in Casas Textiles.

They were worth next to nothing, thanks to the publicity surrounding Renata's arrest and trial, but he didn't care. It was rumoured that Renata's brother was propping her up financially, and Nate didn't care about that either.

He pushed through the building's doors, gave his name at the court's reception and waited for the prosecutor's assistant. He disliked the way that his pulse had risen and the nervous energy that coursed through him. Before the aneurism, he would have thrived from it, used it, but now every change in his body could be a warning sign of something terrible.

He shoved that thought to the back of his mind. Nate had recovered. It was the only reason he'd come back six months ago. He would never have returned if he couldn't have done it seamlessly. His reaction times were only a little slower than before, but he was still healthier than most.

'Mr Harcourt?'

Nate turned to find a suited man with glasses peering up at him.

'Señor Torres?'

The man smiled. '*Sí.* It's nice to finally meet you.'

Nate nodded in acknowledgement. He didn't need nice. He needed this done.

'It will all be very simple. The prosecutor will ask you to state what happened, the defence lawyer may have a go at putting a twist on things, but really, with the corroborating witness statements…' Torres punctuated his sentence with an expressive shrug that implied it would be nothing short of impossible for Renata to wriggle out of this.

Nate listened as he scanned the faces of the people gathered in the large foyer.

'Are you looking for someone?'

Nate paused for a beat. He had been and hadn't even realised it. 'More like hoping to avoid someone, but I doubt they'll be here.'

'I can check if you like?' Torres offered.

'No, that's okay. They'll be a witness for the defence.'

'Then there is no reason that you will see them today,' Torres reassured him. 'This way?' It was an invitation Nate couldn't refuse.

The courtroom was situated off a long bright hallway, down which people stalked with businesslike efficiency.

That focused energy was familiar to him and he used it, harnessed it, before he entered the room.

In his mind he'd always imagined his confrontation with the Casases taking place in a London court, with all the grandeur of rich mahogany, green leather, black robes and grey wigs. So the overwhelming use of pine in the small Madrid courtroom left him feeling a little disappointed. Led quietly to a seat near the door, he stared at the back of Renata Casas's dark hair, her shoulders drawn in a line of barely suppressed tension. He glanced at her hand where it rested, white-knuckled, on the pale wooden desk before her.

No, not tension. Anger.

He huffed out a laugh. The audacity of this woman was absolutely outrageous. Conversations between the lawyers and the judge in Spanish washed over him as he took the time to observe her. Occasionally she would lean towards her lawyer and say something and he would nod. Nate wondered how much of that was staged. He looked back over their encounters, and wondered how he'd missed it. How he'd been so taken in, first by her and then by her daughter.

And if his pulse spiked at the thought of Gabriella he chose to ignore it, because his thoughts had flown to that familiar doubt. Had the aneurism already been affecting his actions then? He'd been assured by doctors that it hadn't, that it wasn't how aneurisms worked, but Nate was a man utterly used to, and dependent on, trusting his instincts, trusting only himself.

He'd had to be. Because after his parents' death when he was twelve, after his grandfather had separated him from his sister, he'd been sent away to boarding school, where he'd only had himself. After only days in the cold, feral environment of boys cut from their families too soon, where weakness was a vulnerability to be exploited and grief was something to be repressed, he'd learned that lesson hard and fast.

In the last two and a bit years, that core sense of inner strength had been in question and now it was time to get it back.

'Mr Harcourt?' Torres gestured for him to take the witness seat.

Gabi's heels clicked along the hardwood corridor outside the courtroom where her mother was standing trial. Thankfully, the press that had swarmed like flies on carrion at the start were currently distracted by a politician who had been caught having an affair with a younger colleague and Gabi had managed to arrive unscathed.

She took a breath, trying to level her breathing. She'd meant what she'd said to Javi—she was ready to give evidence against her mother. But she couldn't help that for more than the first two decades of her life, Gabi had clung to the belief that one day, just one day, her mother would explain that she hadn't meant to be so selfish, that she hadn't meant to behave so badly…that she *did* love her.

Gabi had been waiting for something that would never come. And eventually all the tantrums, the way everything had to revolve around her had become so intrinsically part of Renata that she had started to do illegal things, thinking she could get away with it. But in the end it was the emotional manipulation that had hurt the most. Her mother had made Gabi feel that she needed her, that only Gabi could understand her, only Gabi could help her. So she'd stayed, she'd tried. But even that hadn't been enough for Renata's insatiable selfishness.

Gabi wondered if things might have been different if her father had remained in the picture. If he hadn't remarried as quickly as possible and begun a new family—one that suited him better. If she'd had his support, maybe she'd have been able to defend herself against her mother before that terrible last day. But she hadn't.

Gabi turned at the end of the corridor, bending the direction of her thoughts away from such painful meanderings and instead checked her watch. Emily had taken the kids to the museum. A small smile pulled at the curve of her lips. At eighteen months, they were probably a tad too young to take it all in, but she desperately wished she were there with them, rather than here.

But it was time. Time to put it all behind her. For so long, the court case, the fear that she might bump into *him*, had been hanging over her like the sword of Damocles. She'd half expected him to drop into her life and cut it in half. Because beneath her worry about giving evidence against her mother, what had really been chipping away at her nerves, her appetite and her sleep had been the fact that here, finally, was the opportunity to let Nate know that he was a father.

Gabi pressed a hand to her stomach just at the thought of it. She'd wanted him to know for so long. But she'd been alone the whole way through her pregnancy and then when the twins were born. She'd been alone when she'd held them for the first time, seeing the utterly incredibleness of them and not being able to show him. She'd been alone when she'd looked at her children sleeping beside each other and realised what they were: the two pieces of her heart.

The hand against her stomach turned into a fist. She'd been alone on the long, lonely nights when both the twins were crying inconsolably, and she'd been alone when she'd *needed* him, and she'd still tried to reach him. But on their first birthday she had drawn a line, promising that she wouldn't open them up to the same devastating rejection that she had experienced herself.

But now that Nate was here, in the flesh, could she keep that from him? It made it different, didn't it? She *had* to tell him now.

Señor Torres opened the door to the courtroom and peered around, smiling when he found her. He beckoned her towards him and Gabi refocused. One thing at a time. It was how she'd managed to survive the twins' first year. And now their second.

One thing at a time.

Gabi entered the courtroom and took the seat at the back that Señor Torres indicated for her, keeping her gaze low while her pulse raced, terrified of meeting her mother's eyes. She hadn't seen Renata since that night. They'd had no correspondence, her mother unwilling and Gabi simply unable to face the mother who had called her such horrible things. The terrifying *jealousy* her mother had revealed that night, even after intending for Gabi to 'sway' Nathanial Harcourt to blindly hand over money for shares Renata couldn't provide. The hatred. *That* was what she'd seen that night. Her mother had hated her. Gabi struggled to take a breath around the emotion clogging her throat.

'Thank you for explaining the minutiae of the accounting details,' one of the lawyers said in English, snapping Gabi's gaze up from the floor to the man in the witness chair. 'For the purposes of understanding the emotional impact this had on you and your business, can you describe how the incident made you feel?'

Gabi's heart thumped once, hard, and then stopped—as if it had utterly exhausted itself at just the sight of Nathanial Harcourt. She took in his appearance as he paused to collect his thoughts before answering the lawyer's question. And in that time her eyes saw things that she felt soul-deep—her children's gaze, her son's forehead, the spark of determination her daughter would get...

But there was something slightly different about him. The way he held himself, perhaps? He'd lost weight, but he wasn't gaunt—*lean*. The sense of restrained power beneath the sophisticated handmade suit was irrefutable. The pale blue tie served only to contrast with the rich golden honey of his skin tone. Memories of the night they'd shared pressed at her from all sides until Nate finally answered the lawyer's question.

'This whole situation has been deeply unpleasant. To have my name brought into such a scandal, the name of my family linked with fraud and embezzlement? Untenable. Devastating. If I had thought it a mistake, then of course I would have tried to find a reasonable solution,

but the sheer intent, the meticulous and devious planning that went into defrauding a foreign businessman?
It should be the shame of Spain and if I never meet another Casas as long as I live I'll die a happy man.'

Every single word struck a blow, severing the fragile
hope Gabi had nurtured secretly in her breast. She knew,
categorically and without a doubt, that there was no
way this man would ever show her, or their children, a
kindness and she just wouldn't risk it. She had promised
to protect her children at all costs, and if that included
protecting them from their own father—then so be it.

When Nathanial Harcourt decided to go all-in, he went
all-in. It was imperative that he resolved this situation
conclusively. Because only once this was resolved could
he finally begin to get the rest of his businesses in order.
Yes, he could almost feel it. Things slotting into place,
peace being restored.

And then he looked up to the viewing seats and
caught sight of Gabriella Casas and his entire world
turned on its head.

He watched the blood drain from her face, leaving behind two streaks of red across cheekbones sharper than
he remembered, making him feel like a bastard. He had,
obviously, been directing his statement towards Renata
Casas. But while he couldn't, didn't, know how involved
her daughter had been in the fraudulent plans, he could
see that his words had affected her greatly.

'Thank you, Mr Harcourt, you may leave,' the lawyer concluded in English this time.

Nate stood, unable to take his gaze from Gabriella,

who, it seemed, was equally unable to look away. Help-less. She looked helpless, he thought as he crossed the bright wood floor, utterly uncaring of the conversation passing between the two lawyers and the judge behind him. He ignored Renata utterly, instead taking every-thing in about the woman who had bewitched him over one single night—the *only* woman he had let his guard down for.

Oh, he might be world-renowned for the company he kept on his arm and in his bed, but that was a long time ago now. Gabriella was the last woman he had been with and at the time he'd been taken in by what he'd thought had been honesty. He was so lost between his memories of that night and the way that Gabriella was looking at him now, he was completely ignorant of the commotion building behind him.

All he could see was her large eyes, reminding him of labradorite, watching him walk towards her, the slashes of shame and something else making a mockery of the way she had flushed with pleasure, the sprinkle of freck-les he remembered across her nose dimmed by her pal-lor. Her glorious hair, silken strands he'd fisted in his hands to bind them together, was hidden, pulled back harshly from a make-up-free face. She looked dimin-ished, less than, and something in him roared in denial that he might have had some part to play in that.

No, it was a ruse, he told himself. As he drew closer, she rose from her seat to meet him and if there was something awkward about her movements he didn't no-tice it, because he was lost in the memory of how per-fectly they had fitted that night. How he'd let himself think, believe, that for once he'd found someone who might actually understand him. Might actually want him not for his money or his status, but *him*.

He opened his mouth to speak when he suddenly heard a cry behind him.

If the last few years had taught him anything, it was how to differentiate the sounds of pain. There were cries of agony, hurt, frustration, fury, injustice and desperation. But the sound that Renata Casas had made was none of those things. It was indignant. Selfish. Outraged.

Before turning around to see what had caused Renata to make such a noise, he caught Gabriella paling even more, closing her eyes as if warding off a wave of pain. Frowning, he glanced back to find Renata Casas glaring at him and her daughter, together, just before she collapsed into the most dramatic and ridiculous faint Nate had ever seen.

The court had been adjourned for twenty minutes when Renata's defence lawyer insisted that his client be assessed by a medical professional. The prosecution and the judge seemed to have very little patience for the entire thing, but agreed with the need to determine that the defendant was at least legally fit to continue.

Señor Torres had ushered Nate and Gabriella back out into the hallway to wait until a decision on how to proceed had been made. Gabriella had immediately taken out her mobile phone and started to type furiously back and forth with someone and, while her phone was on silent, the increasingly frustrating sound of its vibration was beginning to grate on Nate's nerves.

Was it a boyfriend? A lover?

He pulled himself up short, startled by the sting of jealousy burning its way up his spine. He turned on his heel to face her, unable to hold his curiosity back any more.

'What are you doing here?' he demanded.

She bit her lip, but kept her gaze firmly on the screen of her mobile. 'I'm here to give evidence.'

He braced his hands on his hips, staring at her, willing her to look up at him. 'But it's the prosecution's turn for witnesses.'

'Yes.'

'Yes, what?' he demanded. Why was she being so difficult?

Finally, she looked up at him, her gaze clear of the anger and frustration he felt pouring out from him.

'I'm giving evidence against my mother.'

'What?' Shock cut through him.

'I had thought,' she said carefully as she put her phone away, 'that you were much quicker than this. Maybe your…' she trailed off, her hand gesturing in the air as if looking for the right words '…"sabbatical" has affected you somehow?'

He ground his teeth together to prevent the angry retort on his tongue from emerging. Her words had hit a little too close to home. This woman was *nothing* like the sweet, funny, guileless girl he thought he'd met. She might be giving evidence against her mother—she might be helping his cause—but that didn't mean she was innocent of any of this. He *would* find out her intentions here.

* * *

Gabi's pulse was racing and her blood was boiling. How could she have *ever* spent a night with this man? He was arrogant, presumptuous, *estúpido*. The only satisfaction she'd had from their encounter was seeing that her reference to his slow wits had hit home. She was pretty sure that not many people managed to get a strike against Nathanial Harcourt.

Her phone vibrated in her hand.

We're outside.

She stood, suddenly desperate to get herself and her children as far away from Nate as possible.

She nodded at him. 'Mr Harcourt—' and half fled down the corridor.

'Is that it?' he called after her. 'Really?' he practically yelled.

Really.

Señor Torres would message her to let her know when she'd be needed, but Gabi knew her mother. Knew what had driven her outburst today too. She hadn't missed the way Renata's eyes had widened in realisation as she'd seen the two of them together, what that meant for the grandchildren she knew about but had never met. But, more importantly, what that meant she could use for her trial.

A hand tightened around her stomach, warning her that whatever had happened today wasn't over. There would be repercussions, she was sure, but for now Gabi just wanted to hold her children and take them all as far away from here as possible.

She practically ran down the stone steps, unable to shake the feeling that something was catching up with her, gaining on her. But as she burst out into the sunshine and onto the pavement, the fresh air blew through the sense of claustrophobia. She gathered herself quickly, refusing to let the twins catch on to how rattled she'd been, not only seeing her mother but also their father.

'Mamá! Mamá!'

She turned, instantly recognising her son's voice, and swept Antonio up into her arms. She adored the way he loved her, unrestrained and uninhibited. She cradled his head to her neck and looked to Ana, so much more stubborn and independent than her brother, but just as loving. Her heart swelled. She didn't need anything more than what she had, she told herself. Not Casas Textiles, not her mother and certainly not Nate.

'I'm sorry, I kept them away as long as possible,' Emily said, her daughter in a sling nestled against her chest. 'But Antonio wouldn't settle.'

'That's okay. Thank you so much for taking them in the first place,' Gabi said, settling Antonio on her hip and reaching for Ana's mop of curls.

'Did something happen? You're out earlier than I—'

Gabi saw the concern in Emily's gaze before her sentence trailed off and turned to see what she was staring at before she could stop herself.

Nathanial Harcourt stood at the top of the steps, his jaw clenched, his jacket open and riffled by the breeze. The thick blond swathe of hair shadowed his brow, but nothing could mistake the intensity of his gaze as he observed Gabi with her children. Even from here, the taut lines of his body were forbidding, and Gabi had the sudden urge to flee.

'Gabi?' Emily asked.

'It's fine. We just need to go. Now.'

For six hours Gabi felt as if she were on the verge of a heart attack. Panic had taken up residence in her chest and only when she got back to the little villa that was nestled in between Nerja and Frigiliana did she finally feel that she might have outrun her past.

She had opened all the windows in the villa and filled the fridge with the food she'd bought on their way back from the small airfield Javier's jet had landed in. She'd begged off spending the night with her brother and sister-in-law, just needing a little alone time with her babies. Just needing a little alone time for herself.

As it was, Ana had started to cry the moment they'd walked away from their little cousin Lily and it had taken nearly two hours and four books, all the kisses and cuddles feasible, to calm her down. And even then Gabi was half convinced that she'd just exhausted herself to sleep. Thankfully, Antonio had recognised that his mother was at the end of her tether and kindly suppressed the desire to mirror his sibling.

After putting a wash on, and grabbing a few paltry mouthfuls of *tortilla*, *jamón* and *Monte Enebro*, she tackled the washing-up, brushing the tendrils of hair back from her face with suds-covered hands.

She'd made it home without him knowing. The relief, so strong and so sure, swept her concerns finally away, so that when the knock on the door sounded she genuinely thought it might have been Javi checking up on her, or one of her neighbours, who often took in parcels for her.

But when Gabi opened the door to see Nathanial Harcourt standing, with one hand braced against the stone arch and the other fisted at his side, dark eyes bright and sparking with dangerous gold flecks, she was utterly and completely stunned.

'What are you doing here?' she asked, finally finding her voice.

Nate glared at her with a flinty gaze. He opened his mouth as if to answer her question and slammed it shut again before he could.

Gabi's body shivered as goosebumps scattered over her skin. He looked…incredible. Perhaps it was because earlier, back in Madrid, she'd been expecting him, prepared for the sheer might of his presence. But here? In her little home, her sanctuary, it hit her with full force.

He drew from her the kind of response she'd only read about in story books, seen on TV and felt in person only once in her life—the night they'd spent together. It started with a rush that flooded her from head to toe, like a wave that crested over her skin, drenching her in a heat that burned but didn't leave a mark. It prickled her hair like static and snapped at her fingers like firecrackers. And she'd have thought she were going mad if she wasn't almost one hundred percent sure that he felt exactly the same way.

'How did you find me?' she asked, forcing herself to

speak again to break the inexplicable connection that
had formed between them.

'I have people for that.' His voice scraped gravel over
her sensitised skin.

'What do you want?' she asked, her voice trembling.
It wasn't a physical fear—not for a minute did she think
she was in physical jeopardy—but there was a threat
here and it was very real.

He barked out a laugh, as if something she'd said was
funny, and she knew. She knew without knowing, she
knew despite her heart still hoping. He had taken one
look at Ana and Antonio and he'd known.

'Lie to me and tell me they're not mine,' he commanded. 'Do it, and I swear you'll live to regret it.'

CHAPTER THREE

NATE WAS HOLDING on by a thread.

Three things had happened when he had watched Gabriella on the court steps earlier that day.

First, he'd realised that he might have been wrong about Gabriella's involvement in Renata Casas's machinations, though he couldn't be entirely sure that the fact she had been due to give evidence against her mother wasn't just another Casas ploy to escape punishment.

Second, he'd registered with a shocking twist of jealousy and a terrible sense of loss, that Gabriella was now a mother. And he couldn't account for why he suddenly felt as if something precious had slipped through his fingers without him even realising it.

But then, third, when he'd seen the second child, when Gabriella had turned to look up at him, he'd seen fear and secrets in her eyes. She hadn't wanted him to know about her children. *Twins*. A girl and a boy, with eyes just like his and his twin sister's.

The shock had left him standing like a statue on the courthouse steps, long after Gabriella, her friend and the children had gone. With shaking hands, he'd punched in his lawyer's number and ordered him to pull up everything they had on Gabriella Casas, calling himself all kinds of stupid for not doing so before. While his lawyer was doing that, he'd ordered his driver to take him back to the airstrip where his private jet was waiting. Because he didn't have to wait until his lawyer called back. He *knew*, without needing confirmation. He didn't even need to be told the age of the children. Because it was Gabriella who had given herself and their children away.

By the time he arrived at the private airstrip, he had Gabriella's address, a detailed biography and some highly illegally obtained files on her two children. Nate hadn't asked for it, and wasn't sure he even wanted to look at those files, but he couldn't stop himself from staring at the pictures taken by the private investigator hired by his lawyers as early research for the court case against Gabriella's mother.

The short flight south from Madrid to the private airfield near Nerja took less than an hour. Which was precisely how long it took for an atavistic, primal need to see his children to take root. Because when he'd first seen the tiny children it had been as a stranger and now, powerful and driving, terrifying in its intensity, he needed to see them with a father's eyes.

With a start, he realised he'd arrived at the same private airstrip two years ago and directed his driver straight here, ignoring how that made him feel. And now, as he looked down at Gabriella, he was barely holding on. He could see the concern in her gaze, fear even, but honestly, in that moment, she wasn't his concern.

They were.

'I want to see them,' he ground out from between clenched teeth.

She shook her head, sending long curled tendrils of hair flying. 'They're asleep.'

'I don't care,' he snapped.

But the effect on Gabriella was instantaneous. Drawing herself up to her full height, her hazel eyes gleamed. 'They are asleep and I will not wake them. It took hours to get them down.'

'Why? Is something wrong?' he demanded urgently.

Gabriella frowned. 'No. They are just...*tired*,' she stressed.

Ready to dismiss her concern, he stepped forward, only to meet a firm hand against his chest, stopping him.

Gabriella took a visibly shaky breath. 'We have things to talk about, yes. But you do not come into my house with this much anger. I won't have it around my children.'

'*Our* children,' he practically seethed. She didn't respond. That didn't make him feel any better, but he did see her point. He turned away to gather himself, unable to do it under her watchful, determined gaze.

He was getting this all wrong. He knew he was. But how to explain it? This feeling flooding his body like adrenaline, fear and love all at the same time? The fear that something could have happened to them without him knowing, without him being able to prevent it. The fear that something still might.

He turned back, needing to know. 'Would you have told me? Would you have ever told me?'

Everything about her changed in a heartbeat; her pallor turned red as blotches appeared beneath the delicate tan of her skin. Her eyes, glittering shards of defiance, turned dark and forbidding.

'Is that a joke?' she spat.

Nate reared back in shock. Gabriella, as if a red haze had descended around her, stepped forward seemingly without realising it.

'I asked you a question. Is. That. A. Joke?'

'No,' Nate said, holding his hands up as if to ward her off, shocked at the vehemence in her tone.

'I tried to reach you for nearly two years.'

Oh, God.

His stomach dropped the moment he realised what must have happened.

'Every single day, I sent you two emails, I called you on the number that you gave my family three times. I reached out to colleagues who might be able to get a message to you. I reached out to every single one of your companies on public emails, contacts through contacts, uncaring of how utterly delusional it made me look. At one point I thought people were actively trying to conspire against me.'

Nate wanted to bury his head in his hands. They had been, in a way. She had tried to reach him for almost the same amount of time that he'd been sequestered in a Swiss hospital. So no, she wouldn't have been able to reach him. Of course she wouldn't.

'Nate, for the entirety of my pregnancy and the first year of my children's lives, I tried to tell you in every single way possible.'

He clenched his jaw, the muscles aching and throbbing in protest.

* * *

'Where were you?' Gabriella asked, the anger diminishing as she ran out of words, leaving her feeling drained and shaky and strangely vulnerable. 'Where were you?' she asked again, and this time she felt tears press against her eyes as she swallowed them back. *When I needed you.*

Does it even matter? she asked herself. Was there any excuse that could make up for how alone she had been for all those days, and the months that had followed?

Nate's entire demeanour had changed. There was sorrow and guilt in his gaze. He reached for her, but she turned away. No. He had missed his chance with her. She had promised herself that she would never go seeking what wasn't there to be found. She'd learned that lesson directly from her father. So no, Nate didn't deserve her understanding. But, she thought, taking a trembling breath, he *was* the father of her children and he did deserve to see them. She knew that much at least.

'If you have calmed down, you can come in, you can see them but, *por favor*, don't wake them.'

She felt Nate follow behind her, uncomfortably aware of the space that he took up in her home. He was tall and broad, and although she vaguely remembered thinking that there was something different about him, it didn't seem to have affected the impact he had on her.

She led him through the living area and kitchen, doubtful that he'd be impressed with what he saw. Javier had wanted her to have more, but Gabi argued that this small villa was enough. She had refused his largesse, but had welcomed the riot of plants and pictures Emily had insisted would survive a single mother's lifestyle. They had become the bits and pieces that had made this small but perfect villa a home for her and her children.

A home without a father.

She led him to the twins' room, where the door was already open a crack. She turned and found Nate looking almost terrified, and fought the ridiculous urge to reassure him. He had brought this on himself as much as she had. And then she felt bad for her uncharitable thought. She placed a finger to her lips and gently pushed the door open wider.

A nightlight glowed warmly, warding off complete darkness, and Gabi tried to see what Nate saw when he looked at his sleeping children. Long dark lashes spread shadows across round cheeks. Little perfectly formed mouths looked like drawings from a fairy tale and tiny hands flexed in dreams as their chests rose and fell with beautiful regularity. Antonio snuffled a little and Ana was out for the count, as always. Her deep sleeper. It had saved Gabriella's sanity in the months when Antonio was restless and miserable.

Her heart had hurt at the time, and she'd never been able to shake the feeling that even then, even utterly unconscious of how the world should be, Antonio had known that out there was a father who wasn't with him.

Gabriella clenched her fist as she watched Nate stare at his children with something like awe, like love. Was it that easy for him? To come in here after all this time and just be a father? Gabi hated the twist of resentment and tried to turn away.

'Which…' Nate swallowed visibly. 'Which…'

Anger turned to pity in an instant. 'Ana is on the left. She sleeps like the dead. Her hair is just a shade lighter than Antonio's, though you'll not be able to see it now. Antonio, he's the light sleeper. He'll wake up if a pin drops,' she said around a smile, her whisper dropping to an even quieter level, in case she conjured him from sleep. 'Ana is stubborn and determined. Antonio is happy and easy-going, but…'

'But?' Nate turned, his head close to hers, closer than she'd realised.

'But a little more delicate,' she said, suddenly worried that he might not like that about his son. Might want to mould him in ways that went against the beautiful little boy he was. And, just like that, she realised how dangerous it was to bring a stranger into their lives. A stranger who had power and money that she simply didn't have.

Nate nodded, the darkness of the room preventing her from seeing how he had interpreted her descriptions of their children. *Their* children.

Suddenly she wanted Nate to leave, wanted to put space between him and the twins. She turned away, hoping that he would follow. He seemed reluctant, but at last he came back out into the hallway and followed her into the large kitchen.

'Would you like a drink?' she asked as she saw that he registered the baby monitor plugged in by the fridge, the half-done washing-up. Signs of a life that had been perfectly fine until he'd shown up.

'Whatever you're having,' he replied tonelessly.

'Well, I'm having a herbal tea, so—'

'That's fine.'

His tone, the absence of one, grated on nerves so frayed she could barely stand it. She wanted to know where he'd been, what he wanted. Was he planning, even now, to take her babies away from her? Did he have that right? Surely a court would side with her.

Sí, cierto.

Gabriella Casas—the daughter of a woman currently on trial for embezzlement and fraud. Fraud that her mother had tried to implicate her in, determined to shift the blame away from herself.

She hated it, being so vulnerable to him, but there was no doubt in her mind that she wouldn't be able to stop him if he decided to turn against her. Everything she had done in the last two years had been for her children. Everything she would do for the rest of her life would be about them, about ensuring that they were raised in a better environment than she had been. And she would do whatever it took to keep that promise, but…

'Nate…' she turned, her heart in her throat, her eyes filling with unshed tears '…please don't take my children from me,' she begged.

As he'd looked at his children—*his children*—a wave of something entirely foreign, other, but all-consuming had washed over him, changing him on an almost cellular level, so it took him a beat to register Gabriella's words.

'I… That's not why I am here,' he said eventually. And it wasn't. As someone who knew how devastating it was for life to change in an instant, he would never do that to his children.

Not immediately and not without knowing more, at

least. Because although he'd spent one incredible night with a stranger who'd become pregnant with his children, he still couldn't trust Gabriella Casas at all. She had lied to him about who she was—or…at least hadn't actually told him. She had apparently tried to reach him, but what evidence did he have? He knew nothing about her as a mother and if she proved in the least bit neglectful then he'd have absolutely no compunction about removing the children from her care.

But the entire house spoke its own truth. There were child gates across open arched doorways, safety plugs over sockets. There were toys everywhere, softness and love. There were pictures on every single wall. Of Ana and Antonio, of her with them, of her brother and sister-in-law and their little daughter. Pictures *without* Renata Casas, or Gabriella's father—Lautaro, he remembered from the file.

Or himself, he realised with a thud of his heart.

And even if he hadn't been able to take all that in, the report from the PI had been thorough. Gabriella was frugal with her brother's money, had no external income, and had lived life as a single mother, utterly and totally orientated around the twins. She took them to a local playgroup once a week, seemingly just to socialise the children. Had coffee with the other mothers occasionally and, aside from Javier and his wife, Gabriella rarely left the house. Her life revolved around her twins.

Their twins.

Christ. He was a father.

It was something he'd never wanted or intended. He'd never planned on having a family or a generation coming from him—he'd always imagined leaving that to Hope. It wasn't the pressure or the responsibility—he was the CEO of three businesses and the CFO of an international conglomerate.

It wasn't just an innate mistrust of the female sex and what they wanted from him. It went deeper than that. It went to the heart of what family meant to him—the need he'd have to protect, to safeguard his family and the fear of what would happen if he failed. If he failed in the way that he and his sister had been failed after his parents had died.

But now? It wasn't just some hypothetical *What if?* He *was* a father. And it didn't matter what he had felt or feared in the past. He needed to draw a line between then and now. Because now he had to do better, be better. For them. His children. Children that Gabriella had raised, alone, for eighteen months.

'You are their mother, Gabriella. Nothing will change that. Ever.' He wasn't a complete bastard. 'But I'm their father and I *will* be in their lives.'

The darkness flickered back into her eyes. 'Now? *Now* you do?'

Unease settled in his chest as he realised that he couldn't afford to lie to her about where he'd been and why it had been kept such a secret. There was too much at risk. But admitting such a weakness? He warred with it until tension zipped through his body like lightning and the thunder of a headache rolled in.

'Can we sit?'

Gabriella looked at him for a moment and nodded, turning to pour water from the boiled kettle into two mugs, before leading him outside. She put the two mugs down on the table and retrieved a wireless monitor from her pocket, placing it where they could both see it. The wooden table filled the small tiled patio covered by stars, but Nate didn't care that galaxies filled the sky, where the moon was so big it bathed everything in a milky glow.

Where were you?

No one outside the Harcourt family was allowed to know what had happened. And if he had his way—if the plan he was making at the back of his mind worked—that would *still* be the case. Because only once she had agreed to his demand could he be sure that his children would be safe.

'The day after I returned from Spain…the day after the argument with your mother… I was visiting my sister when I collapsed.' His words necessitated an exhalation, but Nate still felt that tightness in his chest, anxiety pushing outwards at his ribs and lungs.

Gabriella frowned, but didn't say anything.

'I was rushed to hospital, where I was diagnosed with a ruptured cerebral aneurism.'

'A cerebral—?'

'A blockage in an artery in my brain burst, causing bleeding,' he explained a little simplistically. 'The doctors had to open my head—' he gestured to his head and Gabriella's eyes widened in shock '—and stop the bleeding. Which they did.'

Gabriella stared at him for a moment as if lost for words and then he could almost see it, all the thoughts crashing through her mind in the space of a single breath, flushing her skin.

'Was it because of my mother? Was it something she—'

The shake of his head cut off her words. 'It doesn't work like that. It could have been there for years and I could just as easily have lived the rest of my life without knowing about it,' he said with a shrug, despite the fact that, only hours before, he himself had half believed the opposite. He'd seen how much the thought of it horrified Gabriella and, in a strange twist of conscience, had wanted to spare her from that.

'Is it...' Concern had her nearly half out of her seat. 'Do we need to get the twins checked?'

He reached for her and gently tugged her back down into her chair. 'It's very unlikely that it is hereditary, but we will absolutely get the twins checked as soon as we can.' He didn't want to frighten her, but he had already spoken to his neurologist in Switzerland and been reassured by him that he didn't need to rush the children directly to him.

'Are you okay?' she asked.

The question surprised him, the genuine concern in her voice hard to ignore.

'Yes.' He gave her nothing more than that. He couldn't. Because he couldn't trust her yet. And because, if he were truthful, he'd tell her that nothing had been okay since the last time he'd seen her.

Gabi looked at him for a long moment, taking him in. She'd seen it—signs of what had happened to him—

without realising it. Although he looked in the absolute prime of life, his skin glowing that pale honey gold of the British, lips an almost enviable shade of blush, she'd known.

She reached hesitantly across the table to the hair that had grown out in the more than two years, pausing when Nate tensed, but continuing when he didn't stop her. She gently pushed back the thick wedge of hair just covering his brow and beneath discovered the thin silvery shadow of a scar well healed. No one would notice it, probably even if they were looking.

He must have suffered so much—shock, fear. And he'd done it alone?

'Why did it have to be kept a secret?' Gabi asked, not out of anger and frustration at the obstacles that had kept them apart, but as a mother who would be heartbroken to know such a thing had happened.

Nate swallowed, the moonlight dancing across his throat as her gaze followed the movement. 'I'm in such a position, in such a family, that to show weakness would—and did—create a power vacuum that impacted my sister and others greatly.'

'Stock and share prices? Lack of confidence, leadership challenges…' Gabi guessed quickly.

Nate's brow raised into a wry question.

'Whatever you think of my mother—what *I* think of my mother—she was a businesswoman first and foremost for my entire life. I understand a lot more than you may imagine.' The last words were delivered frostily but she couldn't help it. She had always been known as Renata Casas's daughter, Javier Casas's sister, no one imagining that she had a fully functioning brain of her own, desperate to prove her own worth.

She shoved that thought aside and focused on the present. She needed to know where she stood—it was what she had made her anchor point after leaving her mother's house.

'What do you want, Nate?' she asked wearily.

A muscle pulsed at his jaw. Moonbeams danced across his cheekbones and his brow cast shadows across an unfathomable gaze. A patriarchal nose spoke of his rigid determination, stubbornness, but in it she also saw her children, heard their laughter. They had inherited their father's good looks.

'I want,' he said, his voice like gravel, 'my family to be safe.' And her heart eased for just a moment before his next words registered. 'I want—and *will*—be here, Gabi, a part of their lives. I doubt you'd have been able to put my name on their birth certificates in my absence,' he said—warned, even—but her mind had suddenly become sluggish, as if not wanting to understand what it already knew. 'So the quickest and cleanest way to ensure my rights as a parent, as a father, would be for us to marry. Obviously.'

Obviously.

It was a single thud of her heart. The swallow of her breath. She couldn't marry this man. Panic and fear crept across her soul. She stared into his eyes, hoping to see what he was thinking, but garnered nothing other than the impression of absolute determination.

'You could take them anywhere tomorrow and I would have absolutely no recourse, other than months, if not years, of legal wrangling,' Nate said. 'I think the Casas family has been through enough scandal already, don't you?'

Gabriella's stomach roiled and acid bit her throat. 'How dare you blackmail me?'

'Are the stakes not worth it?' he demanded. 'Are our children not worth absolutely anything I can do to ensure that I am there, that they are protected by me, my wealth, my name?'

Gabriella scoffed. 'Oh, this is about money, is it? If money was all a child needed then—' *Then I would have been fine*, she managed to stop herself from saying.

She bit her lip and gathered herself, forcing herself to think. Their emotions were running high, it was only natural. And Nate was at least right about one thing— their children were worth it.

'Children need more than money, Nate,' she insisted. 'They need emotional stability, emotional understanding. They need love and vulnerability and are you in a position to tell me that you can provide *that*?' She was shaking by the time she took a breath. His eyes, shadowed in the darkness, veiled his thoughts. *Mierda!* She took a shuddering breath.

'Of course they need those things,' he growled, 'and I'll try not to be offended that you seem to think me incapable of love and emotional understanding,' he went on, the red slash of heat across his cheeks speaking of his anger. 'But do they also not deserve to have both of their parents with them, both of their love, *as well as* the material support that I can provide?'

Nate's words cast a spell. For the twins' entire lives,

she had walked the tightrope between trying to give them whatever they needed and what her conscience allowed her to take from her brother. Because Gabi had allowed her entire life—and finances—to become wrapped up in Renata and Casas Textiles, she had nothing. Her mother's accounts and assets were frozen, and she knew there was no point in approaching her father for help.

Her father. The man who had disappeared from her life the first chance he'd got. Who had remarried and had the perfect two-point-four family, who would all much rather pretend that she didn't exist. Yet here was Nate, telling her—warning her—that he would do whatever it took to be a part of their children's lives. Her heart hurt from being pulled in so many different directions.

'Yes, I want to give my children their every material need, and yes, I want to give my children the kind of family unit that I didn't have growing up. But marriage? You don't even *like* me,' she accused. 'And I don't know you.'

'These are not insurmountable considerations, Gabriella. And nothing that can't be resolved in time. If we are united in our desire to love and protect our children, is that not already a stronger, more long-lasting bind than any mistaken assumptions about love?'

She hated that he was right. Hated that what he said made sense to her. Hit by a wave of exhaustion, from the day, from the months, from the years of doing this alone, was it so bad to be tempted by the offer to share her load and her love for these children?

'I need more than a good sales pitch, Nathanial. I need

'to know what the rules would be, the reality of what this would look like between us.' Gabriella had spent almost her entire life second-guessing herself and her sanity because of her mother. Renata had demanded everything on her terms, but her terms had changed with the breeze and that kind of insecurity was untenable to Gabi now.

'Let me make one thing clear, Gabriella. There is no us. Not in *that* way, even if we marry,' he warned.

She didn't have to ask for clarification. She knew what he meant, even as shame and hurt crawled across her body, leaving angry red fingerprints on her skin. She nodded, acknowledging his words.

'This isn't a decision I can make right now,' she said, buying them both a little breathing space. 'I need time. And you need to meet your children. When they're *awake*.'

CHAPTER FOUR

NATE HAD LEFT not long after that for a nearby hotel and Gabi had stayed outside, beneath the canopy of stars decorating the night sky, wondering what they—who had seen so much—would advise her to do.

If she agreed to marry him, would she regret it? Or should she try to forge her own way ahead? She honestly couldn't tell. She knew what he'd said made sense, legally and practically, but emotionally it felt like insanity.

But whatever passed between her and Nathanial, her children did need to know their father. How she handled this would affect the rest of their lives and she would not, could not, mess that up for them. She used the number he'd put in her phone before leaving to let him know that they would start slowly with the children. His one-word response was quick and curt.

Agreed.

That night she dreamed of touches and caresses, of breathless sighs and pleasure only half-remembered, safe and secure in a dreamworld where reality could neither intrude nor harm. She woke up hot and flustered, but miraculously before the twins had woken.

She tiptoed across the hall and peered into their room, thankful that they were still asleep. If she was lucky, she might even squeeze in a quick shower. She turned just as a loud pounding sounded against the door, rousing the twins from their sleep with cries of shock and surprise. Gabi bit back a curse, placed a soothing hand on the chest of each of her babies, promising in gentle whispers that it would be okay, before leaving to answer the door, which banged ominously again.

She wrenched it open and hissed at Nate, 'Stop making so much noise! You've already woken the twins—can we let the neighbourhood get some sleep?'

With his hand pulled back, he almost looked comical. *Almost.* He certainly looked good, she thought resentfully, knowing that her hair would be pulled in a million directions, that her skin was still sleep-wrinkled, not to mention the fact she hadn't had a chance to brush her teeth yet.

She turned and let him decide whether he'd follow her or not, returning to the twins' room, where Antonio was showing off his impressive lung capacity and Ana looked on the verge of joining in. Deciding to cut the drama off at the pass, she quickly scooped up Antonio and dipped to place a thousand kisses all over Ana, causing her to giggle hysterically, the sound soothing Antonio's tears.

She looked up to find Nate filling the doorway, an intense look in his eyes. She hated that she noticed the breadth of his shoulders in his Egyptian cotton white shirt, the lean hips circled by a black leather belt, the expertly cut trousers that she could recognise as hand tailored. In her mind, she added just a few tweaks to their design to ensure that the soft material hugged his thighs a little tighter, his backside and…

'What can I do?' he asked.

'Coffee. Please,' she added when her conscience prodded her.

He stalked off towards the kitchen and she counted to ten. Her awareness of him was too much and it was something she was going to have to get over. He'd made that very clear the night before.

There is no us…even if we marry.

And she told herself that if she agreed to his proposal she wouldn't need anything more.

She settled Antonio on the ground, leaving him to cling to her leg as she retrieved Ana from the crib. Shaking off all her hopes of a shower, she took the twins into the kitchen, where Nate was making coffee, the rich, heady scent giving her a much-needed jolt. Antonio, still tugging on the white nightdress at her thigh, stared up at his father cautiously with eyes wide and so similar it made her chest ache.

She crouched down to his level, with Ana still in her arms.

'Ana, Antonio, this is my friend, Nate,' she said in English.

Nate's gaze flew to hers, the frown asking his question. 'I wanted them to be bilingual,' she explained, a strange heat on her cheeks at the response she tried not to read in his gaze, which became a flush of defiance and shame under his scrutiny.

But should she feel ashamed that he had missed so much of his children's lives? She had tried so hard to reach him, only giving up when it had started to take its toll. She had spent her entire life asking to be loved by people—she wouldn't waste her children's lives on the same. But that seemed like a very different matter now that he was standing here in her kitchen.

To her surprise, Nate crouched down to meet them low to the ground. 'It's nice to meet you, Antonio and Ana,' he said.

Antonio leaned to whisper in Gabi's ear, *'He sounds funny!'* and she smiled, a smile which froze on her lips when her son turned back to Nate and gave him one of his best smiles.

Father and son stared at each other and, in an instant, she knew, no matter how much she justified it, how reasonable it had been at the time, that her children had missed this, missed the opportunity to be with their father, and it would be a source of guilt and hurt for many years to come.

Nate felt the change in Gabi. She was beginning to soften towards him, and while that felt like a victory, he barely noticed it because he was so distracted by Antonio and Ana. He couldn't stop staring at them, taking everything in about them—their laughs, their moods, how much they looked like Gabriella. How much he had missed. It was an avalanche of emotion he knew would take time to wrangle into order.

Gabi had advised him to let them come to him. They'd let him know when they'd be comfortable with him picking them up, or how much attention they wanted. He hadn't missed the pleading in her gaze, begging him to give them time to adjust to his presence.

All the while, he was still struggling to adjust to *hers*. He'd valiantly tried to keep his eyes at face level that morning while she'd been dressed in what he was sure *should* have been a perfectly sensible white nightdress. The difficulty was that his memory had no problem adding in the details of what couldn't be seen. The early morning wind had pressed the nightdress against curves his hands remembered, skin his tongue had tasted, a woman his soul had recognised.

Until he remembered Gabriella's betrayal and a familiar anger twisted through him. But even that had gone completely out of his mind when she'd brought Antonio and Ana into the kitchen. And that was the last thing he remembered consciously thinking because after that it had just been pure chaos.

Breakfast had been an intense debate of bananas over blueberries, before a bowl of mashed up wheat thing that looked absolutely disgusting. Gabriella had set up the twins either side of her to give her maximum access and it was a system that seemed to work for the most part, if the state of the floor was ignored. Following breakfast, the children rained down mass destruction on the living area, before Gabriella marched them all off for a short walk and play outside before they went down for a nap. At last, he thought he might be able to talk to her, but she'd spent the entire time making lunch *and* dinner, putting on a wash, folding away dry clothes, then quickly hoovering and tidying the sitting room. He'd asked again if he could help, but she dismissed any attempts. He didn't think it was even conscious—it was just 'easier if I do it myself'. Then the twins had woken, and after changes of nappies, and drinks of water, it was lunch, and then more nappies, and...

It hurt his head just thinking about how she did all this on her own. That she'd *had* to do it all on her own took a chunk out of an already decimated conscience. Because the reality was, it didn't matter how that night had ended, whether he thought Gabriella had been working with her mother to defraud him or not, he should have known, or at least made sure, that there were no consequences...let alone twin consequences.

Yes, he'd been recovering from the operation, but physio and rehab hadn't kept him from a mobile phone or a laptop where an easy search or a single question could have provided him with whatever answer he'd needed.

He'd always been considerate of who he shared his bed with, their pleasure and protection as much a priority as his own. But he'd also always been aware of what drew the opposite sex to him. The name and the money: a gift and a curse. More than a few of his lovers had proved more interested in his wallet than him, so Nate had always kept those he shared pleasure with at arm's length.

Until the night with Gabriella—until the night he'd finally thought he'd found something different. *Someone* different. And it was the savage betrayal of that belief that had shut down his usually meticulous care. But no matter the reason why, it wasn't enough of an excuse. It could never be enough of an excuse to have behaved the way he had to her. Guilt filled his chest, even more so since reading some of the emails she'd tried to send him.

'Nate?'

Gabriella's voice pulled him back to the present and he came into the sitting room to find Ana mid-nappy-change and Gabriella jiggling a sobbing, hysterical Antonio up and down in her arms.

'Can you take him?'

'What? I thought—'

'I know, sorry, but Ana needs changing and Antonio won't stop. Here, just…' Nate wasn't quite sure how 'just' was supposed to cover the first time he was to hold his son as a screaming eighteen-month-old, but somehow he ended up with Antonio in his arms, staring up at him with glistening eyes, red cheeks and snot. Everywhere.

And, for a second, Nate had never felt anything like it. This was his child and for all his protests of not wanting children, not wanting a family—one that could be taken away in the blink of an eye, one that he could be taken away from—he understood. He got it. The connection, the bond, the sense of finding the thing that had been missing from his life.

Had his own father felt this when he'd held Nate and Hope for the first time?

And, from somewhere deep within himself, a tendril unwound and connected him to the parents he usually refused to let himself think of. A wet heat pressed against the back of his eyes and, just as he was about to take a shaky breath, Antonio let out the biggest wail and shoved a messy fist at his face as if to push him away.

'Antonio,' Gabriella chided, but Nate absolutely did *not* miss the vein of amusement in her tone.

'Your support is overwhelming,' he observed tartly, covering the startling moment of sentimentality.

'You're welcome,' she replied sweetly.

'I don't remember thanking you,' he sniped, and she laughed and suddenly everything stopped—Antonio's cries, Ana's fidgeting and his heart. Each one of them just stopped to listen to the sound of her laughter, pealing out into the room with such delight and joy that at first Ana joined in, then Antonio, and finally Nate did too.

Nate watched Gabi make her way towards the kitchen after putting the twins to bed that evening. She was unguarded and looked tired, and he felt like a bastard. He'd just finished reading the last of the emails that the acting CFO had deleted, thinking they were either a prank or from a stalker. When he'd been sent the first ones, last night, he'd promised that he'd read every single one of them. And now he had.

He called her name out gently, cautious of waking the twins, and she came to stand on the threshold between the living room and the patio. He wondered if she knew how beautiful she was, whether she was conscious of the impact she had on him or not. He wavered over the thought that would have been conviction only a day before: that she was doing it on purpose.

He nudged one of the glasses of wine he'd poured for them towards her and only when she saw that he'd brought the baby monitor out did she finally give in to his silent invitation. There was nothing but the sound of cicadas as she waited, unable to hear the loud, wild drumbeat of his conscience.

'I'm—' he started as the word caught in his throat and he had to clear it. 'I'm sorry,' he said, forcing the words through guilt that was thick and stuck to his every inhalation. He stared at his hands, too ashamed to meet her gaze.

'For what?' she asked cautiously.

'For not being there when you needed me to be,' he admitted, forcing himself to look up at her, to show her how sincere he was.

She frowned.

'I read your emails,' he explained.

'All of them?' she asked, clearly surprised.

Nate nodded.

'That must have been hundreds,' she hedged.

'Actually, you topped a thousand,' he said with no trace of humour. 'Wouldn't copy and paste have been easier than individually writing each one?' He tried to joke, but it landed flat. He clenched his jaw. 'The acting CFO blocked them all, thinking they were a…scam. I never saw a single one of them until last night,' he tried to assure her.

'Checking up on my story?' she asked a little defensively and he looked away. He *had* been checking up on her. Because every single interaction they'd had until this moment had been either a lie or a misunderstanding and he was finding it hard to keep track.

'Can you blame me?' he demanded, his own frustration eating into his tone and dismantling whatever détente had settled between them that afternoon. He wished he could call the words back, but it was too late.

He could see it, the warring within her—the same hurt and the same anger. And now he remembered what he'd not been able to before: the devastation he had seen in her gaze when he'd confronted her and her mother. The hurt that made him wonder, hope, that he was wrong about her.

She looked away, taking a sip of her wine, and when she turned back her expression was determined, braced for the conversation they should have had years ago.

'My mother sent me to that hotel to seduce you,' she admitted, her gaze locked onto his.

He sat back in his chair, shocked. 'You admit it?'

'That it's what my mother wanted? Yes. Absolutely. But I wasn't going to do it,' she rushed on to say, leaning forward as if to argue her case. 'I wanted to tell you what she was doing. I wanted to warn you, but then you didn't recognise me and instead you…'

'I flirted with you,' he said, finishing her sentence. Remembering how *he* had approached *her*. How surprised he'd been by the fact she'd seemed almost reluctant to speak to him at first.

He shook his head, marvelling that once again this woman had turned his life on its head. Everything he'd thought for the past two years began to shift on soft sands, only to reassemble with new meaning and new direction. But was she really telling the truth? *This* time?

'Why didn't you tell me who you were?' he asked, his voice dark and heavy. 'Why did you leave in the morning?'

'Because… I didn't think I was blameless in all this. My mother sent me there to sleep with you and I… slept with you.' She shrugged as if it had been nothing to share her innocence with him, as if she thought why she had done it didn't make a difference to him. But it did. Because he wanted to believe her.

He searched her gaze, trying to see what she was hiding, but all he saw was shame and guilt.

'I should have told you who I was and why I was there, before anything happened…and then, after?' She laughed, the sound so helpless that a part of him wanted to reach out to her. 'How would you have believed me? How *could* you have believed that I wasn't part of her attempt to steal from you?'

He wouldn't have. He *hadn't*.

Because even now he could barely believe that the woman he'd met that night was as incredible as he'd first thought. As captivating and beguiling as she'd seemed. The integrity and sense of humour, even if somewhat reserved, he'd enjoyed enticing from her had been something miraculous to him. He'd *enjoyed* her.

But the sense of betrayal he'd felt when he'd discovered her identity—and then when he'd uncovered Renata's plan, it had all coalesced into a conspiracy theory that hadn't seemed that farfetched. And, in truth, it wasn't even that far from what he'd already experienced before from other lovers.

But Gabi Casas wasn't just another lover. She was the mother of his children, so, in truth, it didn't matter what had happened before. All he needed was to convince her to draw a line under the past and start afresh—by wearing his ring.

Gabi reached for her glass, but stopped when Nate next spoke.

'It doesn't matter now,' he dismissed.

It did to her, but she didn't think that Nate would believe her or even want to hear it.

'All that matters is Ana and Antonio.'

On that, they could at least agree. But marriage... The thought made her heart ache. Deep down, even though she had become a single mother with two children, she hadn't lost the hope that one day she might find love, that one day she might find a person to put her first, to be hers, someone who would want to spend the rest of his life with her.

But she would not have that with Nate—a man who wore his distrust of her like a suit of armour. She wouldn't have fancy words or endearments, caresses of affection, looks of lust and desire... No, if she married him, she would be denying herself the only thing she had ever wanted—to be loved for who she was.

But what her children would have, if she married him, was a father who she could see would put them first above all things, who would see to their every need, and who would protect them with the same ferocity that she felt.

A father different to her own.

'I want us to be better,' she said, putting the glass down on the table.

'Better?'

'Better than my parents,' she clarified. 'I want Ana and Antonio to have the best of everything,' she said, taking a breath. 'And that includes having both parents here together.'

She could practically feel the roll of victory that shimmered across Nate's body, even as he tried to leash it. She struggled, feeling as if she were handing herself and her children to him on a plate. But she wasn't. Because she was going to make sure that Ana and Antonio would have more than what little she had been given by her parents.

'I understand that you want nothing between us,' she said, looking away. 'But I have conditions too, Nate, and if you're neither willing nor able to agree to them, then we might as well stop this right now.'

'No,' he said quickly. Too quickly. 'I want to hear your conditions.'

'Whatever we agree, you will be in our children's lives, Nate. But if I agree to marry you, if you are going to be their *father*, their *parent*, then I need you here, present and committed to them one hundred percent. I mean it, Nate,' she warned. 'No business meetings that run over,' she said, remembering standing outside the headteacher's office after school for a mother who never came. 'You will be present at every school event, recital, performance.' Knowing the pain of endlessly searching the audience for her father's face, and never finding it. Knowing the hurt of that useless hope.

He shifted forward in his seat, his face coming into the light, holding her gaze with a sincerity that felt solemn, binding, soul-deep. 'I promise you I will be there.'

Dios, how she wanted to believe him.

'I also need you to agree to stay in this marriage until the twins are twenty-one years old.'

He frowned, as if unsure about the strangely specific stipulation.

'Ana and Antonio will be your only family until they are adults themselves,' she said, her teeth clenching at the end of her sentence to hold back the wave of hurt. She couldn't, wouldn't, let them be second-best for their father. She wouldn't let him place a second family over the needs of his first. The visceral pain that tightened around her heart had not dulled over the years. She had simply got used to it.

'Agreed,' he said—and she chose to believe that the understanding she thought she saw in his eyes was imagined. She knew better than to trust what she thought she saw in people. Renata had taught her that.

Every single day with her had been a lesson in caution, because with Renata she'd never known. And not knowing what she'd find in the next hour, let alone the next day, had created such a deep, intrinsic insecurity that she had only just begun to shake it off just as Nate had stormed back into her life.

'And I need one last thing.'

She could see he was willing to agree to almost anything, right then and there, and it eased some of the fear on her children's behalf. At least he was taking this seriously.

'If there's a problem, I need to know. If you're angry or upset, I need you to be clear because I spent *so* many years not knowing with my mother. Having to guess, having to watch, having to bend and twist and change whenever her mood did. And I can't do that again. I can't do it to myself and I won't do it to my children.'

'Of course. I will tell you and if you need to, ask. Any time.'

'The truth. You'll tell me the truth?'

'The truth,' he replied, and she nodded. 'Marriage would give us *both* legal protection, you know,' he said. 'It's not just for me. There will be no prenup and you would be entitled to half of everything I have.'

She waved it aside, missing the look of shock that passed across his features, as if the matter of a few billion pounds were nothing to her.

'It's about them, Nate. It's only about them.'

'So, you agree?' he demanded. 'We'll marry?'

Gabi nodded, wondering if she'd just signed her life away, before looking at the baby monitor and smiling sadly.

It didn't matter. As long as her children were safe.

CHAPTER FIVE

WITHIN TWENTY-FOUR HOURS Gabi was regretting her decision immensely.

'What do you mean, we have to move?' she asked the next day when he laid down his decree like an entitled king. She was giving the twins their lunch, Antonio shaking his head from side to side in a valiant attempt to avoid a spoonful of mushed broccoli.

'You can't expect us all to live here, surely?' he demanded from where he hovered by the doorway.

She looked around the little villa that had been her refuge for the last two years, seeing only memories of the children's first steps, the first time they'd slept through the night, all the firsts that had made her feel a sense of accomplishment as if she'd climbed a mountain.

'What's wrong with it?' she asked, seeing his demand only as a criticism. Of her. Of her as a mother.

'We need more space. And if we are closer to Barcelona then it will be easier for me—'

She dropped Antonio's spoon on the highchair's tray with a clatter, surprising both Nate and Antonio, and their faces were near mirror images of shock.

'No,' she said, her hand cutting through the air. 'No.

That's it. I'm done. I take it back,' she said, walking away from the table and over to the sink. 'I'm not doing this any more. We're not getting married—'

'Gabriella—'

'Please stop calling me that. Your accent butchers it. *Gabi.* Just call me Gabi.'

She knew she sounded irrational, but she couldn't take it any more. Weeks of stress about the court case, months of stress about him and the babies. The only thing solid beneath her feet was this house, her routine. The playgroup once a week. Her brother and Emily.

'Gabi?' he tried, the word sounding even more awkward on his tongue. 'I'm going to clean up the children and put them down for a nap and we can talk.'

She nodded. 'Yes. Absolutely, Nate, because I'm sure you know how to change a baby's nappy, how to give a baby a bath and where to find the clean clothes.'

He took a visible breath, but she couldn't stop.

'If we go to Barcelona, because it's *easier for you*, and you take me away from my support network here, who will help me?'

'*I'll* be your support network,' he insisted.

'Oh, okay then,' she replied, refusing to hide the sarcasm she felt creeping into her tone. 'Let's try this. I have cracked nipples, some discharge from them. Is that—?'

'Stop! Okay!' he said, his words clipped, urgent and shocked. Finally, he nodded. 'Okay. You have a support network here. I get it.'

She nodded, watching him mentally backtrack.

'Did you…really have cracked…?'

'Do you really want to hear about it?' she asked on a half laugh.

'No-o-o…' He drew out the word, pressing down the front of his shirt as if he were in a business meeting as he sat down beside Ana, who had been gazing curiously between them. 'But kind of…' he said, his head tilted to the side, and it made him look nearly ten years younger. It reminded her of the night they'd spent together, before the misunderstandings and consequences. The night she'd laughed and joked with a man who had let her explore her innocent sexuality with both patience and fervour.

She wanted to laugh now, just as she had then, wanting to let the moment magic away all the anger and anxiety…and then Ana flung a spoonful of homemade tomato sauce across the kitchen.

And it went like that for the next few weeks, seesawing between panic that she'd done the wrong thing and Nate easing her mind.

One quiet afternoon, she and Nate told the children that Nate would be living with them from now, because Nate was their *papá*. They took it in as much as any eighteen-month-old would have, the conversation startlingly easy.

'Papá? Okay.'

They were too young for the emotional drama that would have come with age and experience, with hopes, disappointments and hurts meshed together. And they were young enough to adapt, to take their lead from her, so she forced herself to be as easy around Nate as possible. That didn't mean that there wouldn't be tears and tantrums as they all negotiated the new family dynamic, but she could only hope that she was doing the right thing. That Nate would stick to his promise and that he could be the father she wanted for her children. But only time would tell.

Eventually she'd had to concede that Nate was right about the house. They did need a big enough space for the four of them. And when her conscience had wrangled her, just like it had with Javier, Nate had convinced her otherwise. He was their father; anything he did was for them and they would benefit from it. So when he'd shown her pictures of a gorgeous sprawling villa only ten miles from where they currently were, she suddenly understood what he'd meant. The villa was not only heartachingly beautiful, it had two double bedrooms, two children's rooms and two offices. There was a swimming pool— even with a children's area, unobtrusively gated and safe. The entire space was on a single level in a U shape, with floor-to-ceiling windows showing off the beautiful lush garden in the centre courtyard and hidden from sight was a pool house on the far end of the property.

Gabi smiled, knowing that Emily would fall in love with it immediately. And while there was so much for the children, she could see that there was also something for her in one of those offices and that maybe, just maybe, she might be able to find some time to resume her drawing and designs. It was the only thing that she missed about Casas Textiles.

Of Renata's court case, they'd received a message from Señor Torres, explaining that between the delay tactics of the defence regarding Renata's health and various rescheduling requirements, neither Nate nor Gabi would be required to give statements until at least the end of the summer. Two months at a minimum. In some ways Gabi had felt relieved, but in others she hated that it still hung over her, occupying too much of the time she should have been spending on plans for the wedding.

And now that it was only a few weeks away, her designs had been more and more on her mind. In truth, only one design. Over the years it had changed style considerably, but the wedding dress design she had worked on at college, the design she'd never shown anyone, came into her mind almost constantly.

But she thrust the thought aside. This might not be the wedding she had hoped for, but it would be her only wedding. Whether or not Nate took his vows as seriously as she did, there would be no other marriage for her. No other husband she knew as she looked out over the night sky. She hoped that one day she might get to see her dress, but she doubted it would be on her.

Nate was learning to compromise, perhaps for the first time in his life, and he was just beginning to realise how much his sister, Hope, let him have his way. He'd always been an expert negotiator, which usually removed the necessity for him to have to bend others to his will, but Gabriella—*Gabi*—was impervious to his sway.

He knew it would be difficult for them both to meet in the middle. Everything about this situation was entirely new to him, but he was a fast learner and he was determined. But Gabi seemed to resist him at every turn.

'She's going through a lot, Nate. You have to give her time,' his sister urged. 'As much as you should be giving *yourself* time,' she warned gently.

'I'm fine. I've recovered. I'm having check-ups. I'm doing what the doctor advised.'

Well, mostly, Nate thought to himself.

His doctors had advised that he halve his workload. At least. That had been part of his intention when he'd arrived in Spain—to at least remove Casas Textiles from his portfolio, but that had been put on hold the moment he'd met his children. And as for the other businesses, he was absolutely sure that he could handle them, despite what the doctors thought. He had overcome his aneurism and he had recovered. That was all that mattered.

'I can't wait to be there and meet my niece and nephew,' she cooed down the phone. She and Luca were trying for children, and although they hadn't shared much, Nate knew that it wasn't an easy road for them.

'We'll be there soon. Are you sure you've given Gabi enough time to prepare for the wedding?' Hope asked, and Nate smiled.

'She was the one who suggested the date and the timeframe, Hope,' he said, bristling at the suggestion that he was rushing things. That was certainly what his grandfather had suggested—he'd even had the audacity to ask if Nate had requested a DNA test.

'Okay. As long as you're not being difficult.'

'I'm not difficult,' Nate hotly denied.

'You're right. Not difficult. Just stubborn, autocratic and—'

'I'm hanging up now.'

'Luca says hi,' she called as he ended the call.

Nate smiled, putting his phone away. Luca Calvino had surprised him, but if he could have chosen anyone for his sister it would have been him. A man who could protect her from whatever she faced. Yes, he was glad Hope had someone like him.

Which was why he knew that when he met Gabriella's brother again he would have to tread lightly. They hadn't exactly had the best of starts and they were going to be in each other's lives for as long as he lived, because, no matter what anyone thought, Nate was taking his upcoming marriage vows seriously. Yes, he knew that there were practicalities that would have to be navigated. But they would all simply adjust, he thought, as if he could bend everyone to his will.

He looked over to where Gabi was introducing their children to the new house. She was dressed in a long patterned dress that skimmed across her body in rich ochres, reds and oranges that suited her. She picked up Ana and held out her hand to Antonio and she was beautiful. Utterly beautiful and seemingly completely blind to it. And when she turned to him and smiled, his heart pulled a beat and her smile froze, until Antonio tugged on her dress and she turned back to beam at him. His son pointed in his direction and *boom*, his heart pumped hard as his son looked at him with something close to joy in his gaze. The warmth that spread through him eclipsed all else and Nate knew with absolute conviction that he would do anything to make this marriage work. For them. To protect them. It was his only focus. It had to be.

* * *

Gabi fussed around the spectacular dinner table in a way that Nate had never seen before. They had moved into the villa only two days ago, but Gabi's seemingly endless, somewhat nervous energy had ensured that all the children's things were put in the right places and that her belongings were in her room. His room—in the same wing of the stunning U-shaped villa as hers and the children's—had been almost easy to unpack. Unlike Gabi's photographs and bedspreads and soft materials and large paintings and plants, Nate's room was brutal in its simple bare necessities.

Gabi's interior designer sister-in-law Emily had visited before they had moved in and had spent a day walking through the house and discussing all manner of things that Nate had left to them. But he couldn't argue with outcome. They had made the house a home in the blink of an eye. And while he'd ensured that there were assistants and removal professionals ready to help, Gabi had insisted on doing far too much herself. And the short, sharp put-down he'd been given when he'd asked if she might want to share the load with them had stopped any further suggestions.

But the nervous energy rolling off her in waves now as she looked at the candles and low lighting, the vases of flowers and the profusion of food so delicious it made his mouth water, was beginning to rub off on him.

She passed him to fuss over a napkin and he caught her wrist. Ignoring the shimmer of sparks that scattered across his skin from where they touched, he turned her to face him.

'Stop,' he commanded gently.

'But it has to be perfect,' she said worriedly.

'It doesn't. But it *is* pretty perfect from where I'm standing,' he said, hoping to ease her nerves. He could see how much this meant to her and, after everything that had happened in the last few weeks, he wanted that for her too.

He wanted to cup her cheek, reassure her with his touch, but he wasn't sure he had that right. Instead, all he could offer her was his word. 'I promise to try and make this as easy as possible. I will be on my best, most charming behaviour.'

'You want to try and charm my brother?' she asked, almost laughing. 'I'm not sure how well that will go down,' she observed sceptically.

'Then what do you advise? I will do whatever it takes. And I can be charming. Can't I?' he asked with utterly artificial concern, succeeding in making her laugh this time.

'You have your moments,' she admitted.

'This is important to you,' he observed.

Gabi nodded. 'It's...' The shudder that rippled through her breath was audible to him. 'It's the first time that *I'm* hosting them. Not my mother, or not me in her home, *their* home, but them in *my* home. I want it to be perfect.'

'Did you do that a lot? Host for your mother?' he asked gently, trying to get to the source of her anxiety.

Gabi nodded. 'Yes, but it was always—*This is wrong, that's bad, this should not even be here.* Things would get thrown or broken.'

'Thrown?' Nate asked, shocked at the idea.

Gabi shrugged. 'Renata enjoyed being dramatic. Even more so when it came at someone else's expense.'

'Gabi—'

The doorbell cut off what he was about to say and because she seemed almost relieved, he let it pass for now. But he realised that he really didn't know enough about how Renata Casas had behaved towards her daughter.

He and Hope had grown up with two perfect, loving parents. He'd had nearly twelve years with them and he remembered those times as a kind of idyll. His tall, focused father on the brink of becoming Harcourts next CEO. His mother, bright, beautiful and bold, her interior designer's eyes always sparkling.

The night they had been killed in a car accident had taken something from him. His and his sister's lives had changed irrevocably, in more ways than just from their loss. But at least he had known the warmth of their love, the security of it. Seeing Gabi, the determined mother, the insecure sister, the softness clashing with the steel, he wondered just how much her parents had hurt her.

Gabi hadn't been able to watch the posturing between her brother and Nate. And even as she reminded herself that her marriage was going to be nothing more than a co-parenting contract, she *still* wanted her brother and her husband to get on.

'I think it's going well,' Emily whispered, leaning into her shoulder as Gabi rinsed the wine glasses.

Gabi cast a furtive glance over her shoulder, where the two men were all but squaring off. 'This is what you call going well?' Gabi whispered back, wondering what on earth Emily would think going badly would look like.

Emily shrugged an elegant shoulder, her blonde hair falling down her back in gentle waves. 'Nate, he's English, so he's going to be a little more stilted than you might expect. But he's also a Harcourt.'

'What does that mean?'

Emily frowned. 'The Harcourts have been a household name for generations. The public interest in them is on a par with royalty, and I'm not exaggerating. And it only got worse after their parents' death.'

Gabi would never be able to forget the image of the two twelve-year-old Harcourts, each standing behind a coffin, especially given the frequency with which it was used by journalists whenever Nate or his sister were mentioned in the press. Her heart would fall each time, unable to comprehend just how much that would have shaped Nate's life.

'His sister, Hope, regularly gets vilified in the press, though that seems to have died down now that she's engaged again.'

Gabi was fairly familiar with the intrusive nature of the press, courtesy of her mother—but perhaps not on the same level as Nate had been. And she could only begin to imagine how the press would have presented Nate's cerebral aneurism if they had ever found out.

'Charming, though,' Emily continued, unaware of her thoughts. 'And good-looking too,' she observed wryly.

Gabi laughed off the insinuation, ignoring the way her cheeks heated.

'Gabs, Javier and I have been talking,' Emily said, leaning back against the kitchen sink.

She sounded serious and it caught Gabi by surprise, her heart suddenly rippling into a familiar anxious rhythm. 'Is everything okay?'

'What? Oh, yes, absolutely. It's just that...we would like to gift you your wedding dress. I know, or at least I can guess, that this isn't perhaps quite what you might have envisioned—'

'Oh,' was all Gabi was capable of saying in response. Having buried her dress design in a drawer, she had planned to go to a shop when she next had a free moment and buy something off the rack. She hadn't even thought to ask if Emily might want to come because...because she wasn't used to people wanting to be involved.

Suddenly she saw how, because of that, she had made her wedding seem somehow smaller, less important. Not because of Nate and what had motivated it, but because she had kept it small. The thought that Javi and Emily wanted more for her, wanted it to be something special, brought a damp heat to the backs of her eyes. And that made her brave enough to ask, to hope, that they might agree to her suggestion.

'Actually, I was wondering if I might have one of my designs made. It's nothing, really—'

'Absolutely!' Emily cried, cursing Renata Casas to hell and back for the damage she had done to her children. Gabi had so much potential, but was only beginning to realise it when she'd discovered she was pregnant. Emily had watched as Gabi had navigated that with an emotional integrity and authenticity that would seem impossible to anyone who knew Gabi's mother. But she could only hope that her burgeoning sense of self wasn't lost beneath the powerful character that was Nathanial Harcourt. 'Do you have the designs here? I would absolutely love to see them.'

Gabi and Emily returned from the study, and the way Emily had gasped when she'd seen Gabi's design had given her a much-needed boost. Emily had refused to let Gabi consider anything other than getting the dress made. The Spanish lace was traditional but used in a modern way, the neckline and figure-hugging silhouette dramatic and impactful. But it wouldn't mean much until she saw it in person. Allowing the tenuous feeling of excitement about the wedding to grow as they returned to the dining table, her stomach dropped to find Javier and Nate standing with fists at hips, pointing accusingly, the air heavy with harshly spoken words.

'No. You have it completely wrong.'

'Me? You are delusional, Harcourt. Utterly delusional.'

'That's rich, coming from a man who thinks that—'

'What is going on?' demanded Emily, presumably before either of the two men could hurl any more insults that they couldn't take back.

'Nothing.' Javier shrugged, instantly his demeanour changing to confused.

'Nate?' Gabi asked, hoping for more clarification.

'What?' he asked, seemingly equally confused. 'We were just talking about football.'

'Football,' Gabi repeated. *'Football?'*

'Yes,' both men replied at the same time, as if it were Emily and Gabi who were being particularly dense.

'Football,' Emily said to Gabi, nodding, and grabbed a bottle of wine and two glasses and led her outside and out of the way of the male bonding session.

'Football?' Javier demanded the moment the women had left the room.

'Would you rather I tell them what we were really arguing about?' Nate bit back, pulling his tie a little looser.

'Probably not,' Javier growled. 'Look, Gabi's happiness is my number one priority in this. You, I couldn't care less about.'

'That, you have made painstakingly clear. And I'm fine with it, by the way,' Nate added with a pointed finger. 'But you should know that I feel the same way.'

'You won't tell me where you were for the first eighteen months of your children's lives?'

'I've told Gabi and that she's fine with it is all that matters,' Nate warned darkly.

Javier levelled him with a gaze, seemingly taking Nate's statement as good enough. For now, at least. The Spaniard fisted his hand and pressed it against his lips, seemingly at war with himself over his next words.

'Gabriella… She has been through a lot. It is up to you what she tells you of our mother—but you should know that Renata Casas has not one single maternal or unselfish bone in her body. The woman is a menace. You need to be ready for her.'

'Understood.'

'I'm serious.'

'So am I. You're not the only one with a difficult family, Casas.'

After a beat, something else came into Javier's gaze. Sincerity and something almost like a plea. 'She deserves to be happy, Nathanial. Safe and happy. If you can't give her that, then you should let her go. Now, rather than later.'

He heard Gabi's brother's words, took them in as much as any brother would, but also heard them as a fiancé and the father of Gabi's children.

'She will be. I'll see to it.'

'You better had,' Javier said, before heading out onto the patio to the long wooden table beneath the arched pergola. 'Emily, *mi amore*, pour me a drink and remind me never to try and teach an Englishman about football again.'

Nate chucked out a cynical laugh—he could respect the man, if not quite say that he liked him yet. But he was glad to see that Gabi had a brother as strong-willed and determined to protect her as Nate felt about Hope. Which was why he refused to simply dismiss Javier's warning as the behaviour of an overprotective brother.

Nate quickly fired off a message to his brother-in-law Luca Calvino—the owner of Pegaso, an international security company—asking him to find out everything about Renata Casas, including where she was. Now was not the time for lawyers. This was his future wife and he was taking no risks with her or their children.

Javier was right. From what Nate knew of her, they should be ready for anything. Putting away his phone, he watched Javier, Emily and Gabi talking and laughing amongst themselves, and found that he suddenly missed his sister. This was the kind of family unit that they would have had, had their parents lived, had they not been foisted off on boarding schools and a grandfather only interested in business and strength, might, money and power. In that moment, Nate made a silent vow. To Gabi, to his children. Never would they grow up the same way that he and Hope had. Never.

CHAPTER SIX

GABI LOOKED AT herself in the mirror, turning at every angle to stare—not at herself, but at her wedding dress. It was *beautiful*. It was the first and only of her designs to have ever been made and it took her breath away. Javier had found the perfect seamstress, who had been able to perform a miracle in such a short space of time.

Gabi ran a hand across the wide scoop neck and down the embroidered Spanish net lace that had been used to delicately overlay the ivory silk that skimmed her figure perfectly, so that, rather than being tight and confined, it flowed across her skin in a caress.

With her hair piled up in a bun that was artfully messy rather than accidentally, and the small touches of make-up that accentuated the line of her eyes and the colour of her lips, Gabi dared to hope that she looked suitable to be the bride of Nathanial Harcourt.

But if she was suitable to be the bride of the father of her children that would have to be enough for her, she decided, ignoring the painful throb in her heart.

The dress's skirt fell out in a cascade to form a demi-train at the back that could be pinned for ease of movement, but also to increase the shape. She pinned it up, deciding that the train was a little too dramatic for the simple wedding taking place in the gardens of the hotel at the Viñuela Reservoir. She had visited here with Javier shortly after leaving her mother's house, not yet knowing that she was pregnant, and the incredible view of the lake and mountains, the serenity of it, had touched her deeply. When Nate had asked her where she wanted to get married, she'd known that it was here.

A knock sounded on the door behind her, Emily's voice coming through the wood. 'Gabi, are you decent?'

'Come in,' Gabi called, looking back to see both Emily and Hope Harcourt stop in their tracks with gasps.

'You look...' Emily started.

'Absolutely incredible,' Hope finished.

Gabi's chest swelled as she realised that neither of the two women were exaggerating. The blazing appreciation in their eyes soothed some of the doubts she'd developed from growing up under her mother's painful scrutiny.

'Whose is that dress?' Hope asked, her eyes flickering over the material and the design.

Emily smirked. 'It's hers.'

'Yes, I know that, but I mean—'

'No, it's *hers*,' Emily clarified.

Hope's jaw dropped. 'Really? You designed this?' she asked. 'I want it! No, wait, that didn't come out right,' said the blonde Englishwoman so similar and yet so different to her twin brother that Gabi was still getting used to it. 'As a buyer. I want it as— No,' she said, cutting herself off. 'I'm sorry, we can do this later. You look absolutely amazing,' she said, but Gabi had understood, had realised what her future sister-in-law had said. The

CEO of Harcourts—an international, highly exclusive stockist of designer and haute couture—wanted a dress designed by her? 'But we're going to talk later,' she said, pointing a determined finger at her that reminded Gabi of her daughter, Ana.

Her children had been fascinated by Hope and Nate— as if sensing not only family but familiarity between the two adults and themselves. Just the thought of them made her heart race.

'Where are—'

'They're fine,' Emily reassured her before she could even finish.

'They're with my husband, Luca. It's good practice for him,' Hope said, 'and I promise they really couldn't be in safer hands. But I think I might just go and see them—not because I'm worried, but because my niece and nephew are the most adorable children I've ever met!' she cried, giving Gabi a quick kiss and a squeeze on the arm.

Gabi waited for Hope to leave and smiled at Emily.

'She's nice, I like her,' said Emily conspiratorially.

Gabi nodded. Hope and her husband, Luca, had flown in last night, apologising for not meeting her sooner, as if it had been their fault that they hadn't known about her. Gabi hadn't known what to expect, what Hope might have heard about Renata Casas's daughter. For all Hope knew, Gabi could have intentionally got pregnant in order to trap her billionaire brother.

Gabi had been braced for a barrage of questions and instead she'd got reassurances that her brother wasn't a complete arse. Gabi had seen so much in her eyes—hope that her brother would be happy, hope that they could make it work, instant love for the new members of her suddenly increasing family—that Gabi couldn't help but like her fiancé's sister almost immediately.

'And Javier?'

'Javier is with Nate, getting ready.'

'Making sure he doesn't run away?' Gabi asked wryly.

'Probably trying to pay him to run away,' Emily said, and they both descended into giggles.

'This is no laughing matter, Harcourt.'

'It's my wedding, and if I say that I want you to wear a boutonnière, then you should wear a boutonnière, no?' Nate said, greatly enjoying his future brother-in-law's apparent discomfort.

'But mine is *pink*.'

'Real men wear pink,' Nate said with a shrug.

The quick inhalation told Nate that his taunt had hit dead centre. Javier snatched the flower and shoved it rather indelicately into his buttonhole and, with a glare, stalked over to the room's bar and poured himself a whisky.

'Want one?' he asked.

Nate shook his head. He wanted to be completely clear today.

'Don't need the Dutch courage?'

Nate smiled. 'Not in the least. Did you when you married Emily?'

Something indefinable passed across Javier's gaze. 'When I—'

An urgent knock pounded on the door just as Nate's phone started to ring. Both men stared at each other for a second to process that something was wrong before Nate answered the phone and Javier the door.

'It's Renata Casas,' Luca explained. 'She's here.'

'How?'

'The guys I had on her say that she must have switched cars. They weren't expecting her to do so. It's not good enough, Nate. I'm sorry—'

'Don't be sorry, just don't let her anywhere near Gabi. I'll deal with this,' he said, hanging up on his brother-in-law and turning in time to see that Javier must have been given the same information if the furious look in his eyes was anything to go by.

'You coming?' Nate asked.

'Absolutely,' Javier growled.

They found her out by the entrance to the villa, the beautiful sunshine and stunning water feature speaking of serenity that was being utterly massacred by Renata's hysterics. Nate's Spanish was basic at best and he was half thankful he couldn't understand her from the look on Javier's face.

She was being held at bay by one of Luca's discreet security staff and one from the hotel, both attempting to prevent her from gaining any further ground than she already had.

'Basta!' Javier shouted, calling a stop to his mother's sudden hysterics. For a moment.

The look of relief on the two men's faces would have been comical if Nate hadn't been so furious.

'What are you doing here, Renata?' Nate demanded as the two other men stepped back to make space for him and Javier.

'I am here for my beloved daughter's wedding, of course,' she replied, apparently unable to keep the sneer of disdain from her voice.

'You are wearing *white*,' Javier spat, and for the first time Nate realised that Renata was dressed in what could conceivably pass as a wedding dress.

Rapid-fire Spanish passed between them, hot, angry and too quick for Nate to keep up.

He got between mother and son, gesturing for Javier to back up before turning to face Renata. He looked at her—really looked. The arrogance and disdain and fury dripping from every pore seemed to hit the ground between them like acid. The contrast between how loving, how nurturing Gabi was with their children, that she was even capable of such love, despite being raised by this *wolf*, was nothing short of miraculous.

'I am here for my daughter. A mother should be with her child on such a day as this.'

'You're right,' Nate said. 'Gabi should be surrounded by people who love her on this day. People who want the best for her, who want to celebrate her joy, her happiness with her,' he said, and even though he half wondered whether he himself was capable of giving her those things, he knew categorically that Gabi deserved them. 'People who will be there in her life as she moves forward as a mother, as a wife, and as a woman.'

'See? You understand.'

'I do,' Nate confirmed. 'Just as I understand that you are not, never have been and never will be, one of those people,' he said, stepping closer to her, his pulse pounding in his veins, barely contained fury driving him. 'And I will do everything in my power to make sure that you are never able to hurt her ever again,' he promised.

He stepped back and turned to Luca's man. 'Put her in a car. Take her home. And keep her there until this evening.'

'You can't do that—it's illegal. I'll call the police!' Renata yelled.

Nate nodded. 'You're right,' he said, turning back to the man again. 'Take her phone.'

He turned his back on Renata and ignored her screams of frustration and accusations. He retrieved his own phone, called his lawyer and told him to expect a phone call from the Spanish police and to begin whatever passed for a restraining order in Spain. He also passed on the details of the hotel's security man for a witness statement.

'I'll deal with whatever consequences the police deem fit regarding Renata today, but right now, I have a wedding to get to.'

He ended the call and turned to find Javier assessing him with a steady gaze.

'Did you mean what you said?' Javier asked.

'I always mean what I say,' Nate dismissed, struggling a little more than he perhaps should be to get his racing heart rate under control.

'About Gabi?'

'Absolutely,' Nate replied without a second thought. She was the mother of his children. She would soon be his wife. She and they were his to protect and he would do whatever that took. Whatever.

Gabi found herself looking out at a lake that could be mistaken for glass it was so still, reflecting the majestic outline of the mountains in the distance. The water looked almost turquoise today, as if decorated just for her wedding. But it was the serenity that she most wanted in that moment.

Emily had come here yesterday and turned an already idyllic location into a magical wonderland with her interior designer's eye. A magical wonderland where even witches existed, apparently.

Luca, Hope's husband, came to stand beside her and she smiled sadly.

'You don't have to stand guard,' Gabi said gently.

'That's not what I'm—'

'She's here?' she asked. 'My mother?'

The Italian billionaire side-eyed her as if considering what to tell her before turning back to face the lake beside her.

'Sí,' he said.

Gabi sighed. She was not surprised. Not really. It had been like that for almost her entire life.

She nodded. 'On my sixteenth birthday, she was so insecure about having a "woman" as a daughter that she seduced the father of my best friend and was caught having sex with him in the downstairs bathroom by his wife,' she said, shuddering at the memory, and at the

devastation of losing one of the few friends she'd managed to make at the private school that she'd hated. Hu-
miliation, anger, resentment and genuine self-pity—that
was what Gabi associated with the key moments in her
life. So she had learned to wish them away. Learned not
to have expectations. Learned not to hope.

'I wonder what she had in mind for today,' she said
ruefully.

Gabi had needed time and support when she'd left
her mother's house, staying for a while with Javier and
Emily, finding a therapist who could help her navigate
her mother's narcissism. Narcissism in the true sense
rather than a misplaced character descriptor. It was as
much beyond Renata's control as was breathing. It had
to be about her, always, because there was nothing else
of importance. Not even her children.

Gabi knew she should have continued with the therapist, but when she'd discovered that she was pregnant
she'd switched her focus to them, ensuring that they
would have a mother who put them first. Always.

'Nate and Javier are dealing with her. They will make
sure she leaves.'

Gabi nodded. 'For now,' she amended. 'She'll leave
for now.'

Luca murmured an agreement and there was a peace-
ful silence between them for a moment and she realised
what was different.

'You didn't try to make an excuse for her,' Gabi observed.

Luca shook his head, his lips pulled down. 'I know
about bad mothers,' he said simply. 'There are no ex-

cuses or platitudes for those. Most people look to reassure, to insist that there's some goodness to be found. But sometimes,' he said, looking at her directly, 'there is none. So, no. No excuses for bad parents,' he said, and Gabi wondered if he'd noticed that her father wasn't there either.

He'd sent flowers. A pretty bouquet with a bland printed note:

Wishing you the best on your special day

They could have been sent on her birthday, if he'd ever done such a thing.

What was wrong with her that her parents couldn't be like everyone else? she thought with a vicious twist of hurt. But wasn't that what Luca was saying? That she wasn't alone in the 'bad parent' stakes?

She liked Luca, he was near perfect for Nate's sister, a calm, grounding force that the other woman needed. Nate's family suited him.

'Family is what you make of it,' he said, turning back to watch Emily and Hope playing with the children as the few guests they'd brought together began to take their seats on rows of chairs with white bows tied at their backs. The officiant waited patiently beneath an arch of beautiful flowers and twisting ivy, the lake visible beyond. 'And, from the look of it, you have a rather spectacular one,' he said, and Gabi couldn't help but smile. 'There isn't a single one of them that would not die to protect those children or you, Gabriella,' he said, bringing her gaze back to his. 'And I know what I'm talking about.'

In the distance, Nate and Javier emerged from the

building, wearing sunglasses and looking utterly devastating in their tuxes. Whether they knew it or not, they matched pace and looked for all the world like two mythological gods come to earth to play amongst the mortals. The wind pressed against them, showing them off at their best.

Nate was fiddling with a cufflink, but both his and her brother's attention were fixed on their destination at the top of the aisle. Nate's beauty—the natural power of him—called to her all the way across the courtyard. Handsome barely covered her soon-to-be husband. *This* was the man she had spent the night with in a hotel, *this* was the powerhouse that had confronted her mother in court, *this* was the father of her children and the man she would spend the rest of her life with.

A shiver ran through her at the thought of what kind of wedding night they could have had, and what they *wouldn't* have. But then the sound of her children's laughter was carried to her on the same wind that had pressed against Nate. It was a timely reminder of her reasons for being here today. The safety and security of her children, and the hope—the desperate hope— that they might have a better upbringing than she'd had.

'Shall we?' Luca asked, offering her his arm.

Nate pulled at his cufflink as they made their way towards the aisle, scanning the grounds for a sign of Gabi. He saw his children first, playing with Emily and Hope, his heart missing a beat when Ana looked up at him with large, almost green eyes and a bright smile, and waved at him.

Javier paused at the bottom of the aisle and Nate turned to look at him.

Javier smirked. 'You think I'm going up there with you?'

'That's my job,' Luca announced as he met them, Nate trying to look around him for Gabi.

Luca tutted loudly enough to bring Nate's attention back to him. 'You're going to want to wait to see her, man, seriously. Let's go.' He nodded to the top of the aisle, where a large, intricate flowered arch bowed over the officiant. Nate frowned, and tried to lean around Luca to see Gabi again before being not so gently nudged by Javier.

'Go on, get up there,' Javier said with a laugh, and Nate gave up, following Luca to the top of the aisle.

Shoving aside his frustration with his soon-to-be brother-in-law, he grimly smiled at the few guests he'd wanted and Gabi had gathered, not in the least bothered by how selective they had both been.

Luca passed by Hope and leaned in to give her a kiss, full on the lips, and batted a hand at the *oohs* and *ahhs* that came in response from the people around them. Nate felt an awkward pressure in his chest, witnessing the easy affection between his sister and her husband.

But they had what they had, and he knew what he needed with Gabi. He'd not lied when he'd told her that they couldn't be an 'us'. He simply couldn't risk it because, deep down, he knew that she would make him vulnerable in a way that he might not be able to survive. Yes, he had wants and needs, but that didn't matter. He could—and would—respect the sanctity of marriage, respect his *wife*, and not seek satisfaction elsewhere.

But when the children were old enough? When they were twenty-one, he would let Gabi go wherever she—

At that precise moment, Nate caught his first glimpse of Gabi in her wedding dress and the bottom dropped out of his world.

His heart pounded so powerfully in his chest, he barely heard Luca taunt, 'Told you so.'

He could feel his skin flush beneath his suit, causing a bead of sweat to trickle down his back. He fisted his hands by his sides to stop himself from doing something stupid, like reach for her, pull her to him and—

'Sunglasses,' Luca prompted.

'What?'

'Sunglasses,' Luca hissed.

Nate pulled the sunglasses from his face and caught the moment that Gabi, meeting his gaze, paused ever so slightly mid-stride. He felt it, the arc of electricity that snapped between them, remembered it from the first moment he'd laid eyes on her in the hotel bar and thought for just a second that she'd felt it too, pulling at her, binding her to him just as surely as any vow or legal document. He'd never, no matter how many women he'd encountered before, felt anything like it.

Gabi was unique, the only one, obliterating all thought of anyone else and making a mockery of his determination to keep her at arm's length. She purposely looked aside, trying to sever the connection between them, smiling and nodding to their guests. But it didn't work.

She was utterly exquisite, her hair piled high in a bun with tendrils flickering in the breeze. Subtle make-up only served to accentuate her natural beauty—the tan of her skin highlighting the sea-storm hazel of her eyes. She wore no necklace, no earrings—not even an engagement ring. She didn't need to, because she was the jewel, he recognised in an instant. And while he could vaguely hear mutterings about the dress, *she* shone the brightest.

As she reached the top of the aisle she gave her bouquet to Ana and kissed Antonio, who fussed quietly next to where Emily carried their cousin in a sling.

Look at me, Nate urged silently. *Look at me.*

Because he wanted that feeling again. That thump to the chest as powerful as any punch, just to know he hadn't been imagining it. As a man who knew what it felt like to have two hundred joules thumped into his body to bring him back to life, Nate wasn't exaggerating the impact of just one look from her.

Look at me.

Finally, Gabi straightened, walked up the two small steps to join him, the officiant and Luca on the dais and turned to face him.

Christ.

He hadn't imagined it. He was hit with such force it nearly knocked him off his feet.

He barely took in a word the officiant said that day. Later, people would tell him how beautiful it had been, how touching the service was. But he only had eyes for Gabi. His ears only heard her words and if he'd had even the slightest whim of fancy, he'd have said that his soul only knew hers that day.

'Nate?' the officiant prompted.

'Mmm…?' he said, dragging his attention from Gabi

to hear the gentle ripple of laughter that rolled across the guests.

'Your vows?' the man asked.

'Oh, yes. Vows.' More gentle laughter covered his moment of awkwardness as he came back into himself and what he needed to do. 'Gabriella…' he started, pushing beyond the sound of blood rushing in his veins. 'I could give you someone else's promises—to cherish you until death, to have you, to hold you, but those promises, said by so many people, don't feel right for you or for us,' he admitted, knowing that she would understand. Knowing that she also knew that to speak of love would be a lie, to speak of honour, when he had so little, and cherishing, when he'd promised not to do such a thing, felt like sacrilege.

'So, instead, I will give you this promise. I will be father to our children, I will be with you as we guide them to be the best versions of themselves they can be. I promise to walk beside you in all things, to encourage and help you in all that you do. I promise to talk to you, listen to you and care for you. Through whatever comes our way, I will be whatever strength, comfort, counsel or companion you need. Everything I am, everything I have, is yours, now and for ever.'

There was a moment of such silence he thought he might have lost his hearing, until every guest collectively let out a sigh. Someone laughed, someone clapped, one of the children cried a little before being hushed, but all Nate could see was the tears gathering in Gabi's eyes, and he could only hope that he'd said the right thing, *done* the right thing. Finally, the near stranglehold of anxiety loosened its grip from around his throat and he took his first deep breath of that day.

'Nathanial…' Gabi started, having to clear her throat before continuing. 'Like you, I didn't want to speak another's words today. Your promises suit me and they suit us,' she said, reassuring him a little. 'So here are mine for you. I will care for our children, with you by my side, teaching them right from wrong while allowing them to explore their creativity, self-expression and emotions without judgement or confinement. I will share my thoughts with you, my joys, my sorrows, and hope that you will trust me with your thoughts, joys and sorrows. In sickness and in health I will carry your burdens as my own,' she promised, and his heart flipped in his chest, 'as I know you will mine. Love comes in many forms—ours comes as a family,' she concluded, and the guests, perhaps slightly misunderstanding words intended for him, a meaning only shared by them, descended into rapturous applause.

The officiant continued the remainder of the ceremony and could have spoken Ancient Greek for all Nate knew, but the last sentence rang clear in his head like a bell of warning. One he had absolutely no intention of paying heed to.

'You may now kiss the bride.'

After such pretty words, after such sweet simplicity, the kiss should have been tender, sincere, innocent even. But it was nothing of the sort. He met Gabi in the middle, and any thoughts of the chaste kiss that he had intended fled the moment his lips met hers.

Heat burned the back of his neck, tension fisted his

stomach, and it took everything he had not to reach for her arms and pull her against him, to hell with the guests watching on. In what must have been a state of equal shock, Gabi's lips parted in a gasp, inadvertently giving him access his body took full advantage of.

He felt her submit, almost melt against him, immediately creating an addiction in him that would never be satiated. Craving coursed through every fibre of his being and he couldn't let her go. His hands automatically drew her closer against him, and the thrill of victory cried in his breast as he felt her body press against his. It was only when the whooping cat calls from the audience finally cut through the pounding of his heartbeat in his ears that he paused.

Gently pulling back from her, Nate realised that he had completely obliterated the line he had drawn between them and he would never be able to put it back.

CHAPTER SEVEN

GABI WOULDN'T HAVE been able to say what had happened after the ceremony. Not until she finally found herself sitting at a long table, Ana and Antonio fussing between her, Emily and Hope. Her lips tingled, her heartbeat was erratic, her skin still felt flushed and over-sensitised. Nate had plunged her into a sea of sensation and she was barely able to stay afloat.

Her eyes tracked him wherever he went, her body felt him from across distances near and far. It was as if the kiss had forged an unbreakable connection between them. Not just legally or emotionally, but *physically*. Her body remembered their night together, the passion that had brought her not only so much pleasure, but two children. Through their presentation as a married couple, and the champagne toasts and canapés, she oscillated between memories of kisses, past and present, as if drugged.

Until they sat for the wedding breakfast and Ana put her arms up to Nate in the universal gesture for 'hold me'. Gabi's heart stopped when Nate, staring at his daughter as if she were the most precious gift he could receive, plucked her from Emily's lap and held her to his chest as if he might never let go.

Antonio crawled into her lap, Gabi's arms automatically coming around him as he leaned against her, and both parents looked at each other, their children in their arms, and knew that, no matter what had happened in the past or would happen in the future, they had done the right thing.

Nate came to sit beside her at the double seated head of the table, and she fought the urge to simply rest her own head against his shoulder. Her mouth wobbled in an attempt to prevent the yawn escaping, but Nate's focused gaze saw everything.

'You're tired.' It was a statement, not a question.

'I'm fine,' Gabi dismissed with a patient smile. 'We'll be home soon.'

Something flickered in his gaze, and she was about to question him on it when Javier tapped a fork to a glass and insisted on making a speech. She leaned back and gently rocked her son as her brother welcomed her new husband to the family, as Hope and Emily, and even Luca, looked on with emotion shining bright in their eyes.

Family is what you make of it,' Luca had said.

Words to live by, Gabi realised. And while she had been utterly and irrefutably focused on making sure that she was the perfect mother for her children, the kind of mother she'd never had, she thought that perhaps it was time to ensure that their family was much bigger than her. She looked at Nate, could see the ferocity of his love for his sister, the need to protect those he considered *his*. But she wanted more for Ana and Antonio. And she was beginning to think that they might be able to make that happen.

Nate ended the call that had put the final part of his plan in place. It was an extravagance, for sure, but one that Gabi and the twins deserved. They *all* deserved.

'What are you doing out here? It's nearly time to say goodbye to the guests.'

He turned to find his sister walking towards him across the courtyard, a hand shading her gaze from the late afternoon sun. He looked at her, eyes bright, cheeks pink, and felt relief. He could see how happy she was, how much she'd enjoyed meeting her niece and nephew and the new members of their family.

As she drew closer, she narrowed her eyes. 'What are you scheming?'

'Nothing for you, *dear sister*. Just some honeymoon plans.'

'Honeymoon? I thought you were just returning to the house?'

'Not any more.'

'Well, you'd better be sure about it, *dear brother*,' she said, sweeping her arm around his waist, 'because Gabriella Casas doesn't strike me as a woman who likes having plans changed on her.'

'Gabriella *Harcourt*,' Nate replied with shocking possessiveness.

Hope turned as they entered the large barn where the wedding breakfast had been served, and smiled with something like pride. 'Yes, she is a Harcourt, isn't she.'

Nate looked up to find Gabi once again looking at him. Ever since the officiant had proclaimed that he could kiss his bride, it was as if an invisible thread had bound them together. It was something that pulled and pushed at his skin, wanting and waiting and not in the least bit patient.

He tried to shake off the feeling that Hope's warning was unnecessary as they said goodbye to the officiant and staff, as the last of the guests drove away from the stunning venue, and Gabi looked at him tiredly and said, 'Home,' with such longing he realised that he might have just made a very big mistake.

He winced. 'About that...'

Gabi was fuming. And it wasn't easy to fume on a speedboat slashing through waves, holding onto your children as if their lives depended on it. Yes, they were wearing life jackets, yes, she knew that they were 'perfectly safe', as the pilot of the boat had told her repeatedly, and yes, much to her irritation, they *did* seem to be having the time of their lives. But *she* wasn't.

All she'd wanted was to go home. Where she could change, where she could get the children back into their routine, where there was familiarity and rhythm. She'd thought that she and Nate could spend the next few weeks settling into whatever it was their marriage would look like.

Gabi studiously ignored Nate as he cast nervous glances her way. The arrogant, presumptuous, *estúpido...* What use did she have for honeymoons and husbands? She'd been perfectly fine without him. And then she caught sight of Antonio wriggling in his father's lap, a look of sheer joy across his face as he cried happily into the wind, and bit back the thought. It was right that her children had both their parents—she just wished their father wasn't so high-handed, or handsome.

She hadn't wanted a honeymoon, because theirs wasn't a normal marriage. It wasn't about rose petals and romance, champagne and diamond rings, she thought as she clenched her fist around a ring that was far too much for her, and far too much beyond her wildest imagination. She didn't want a honeymoon because she didn't want to make this longing for something *more* even worse.

The boat arrived at a small private island just off the coast of southern Spain. She'd visited some of the islands during some of her mother's infamously extravagant parties, but Gabi had never been to this one. It looked like a castle rising up from the sea, trees and large boulders simultaneously decorative and natural. She caught glimpses of chrome and glass embedded harmoniously within the wild landscape.

It was beautiful, she thought a little resentfully. It was where she would have wanted to come had she… Gabi bit her lip and forced a smile to her mouth when Ana cheered, looking up at the pretty island.

The boat's pilot guided them efficiently to a jetty and helped them offload as dusk began to descend. Little lights either side of the wooden deck led them up steps that took them towards a house that looked like a modern-day fairy tale.

'What about clothes?' she asked, pulling to a stop halfway towards the villa.

'They were packed and brought here earlier,' Nate replied, leading her on a few steps before she stopped again.

'And the things the children need? Like nappies and wipes, and bottles and toys and—'

'All here, I promise.'

Panic gripped her. 'And Antonio's blanket? He can't sleep without it,' she said, terrified by the hysteria that would ensue if Antonio didn't have his pacifier. 'And Ana, she needs her—'

'Both the blanket and Ana's squeaky clam are here, I promise,' Nate insisted. He held out his hand to her. 'Please, Gabi, just come and take a look. If it's awful, then we can leave first thing tomorrow.'

'Why did you do this?' she asked, unable to keep the utter defeat from her tone.

'Because…' He paused, taking a breath and shifting Antonio onto his other hip, completely unaware of how devastating he looked, dressed in a tux and carrying his son. 'I wanted to do something nice for you.'

With that, he turned and walked on ahead, leaving her to wish so very much that he hadn't.

But, as he had promised, Gabi discovered everything that the children and she would need for at least two weeks in the bags that had been left by unseen staff in their rooms. Ana's toy clam, Antonio's blanket—everything.

Dead on her feet, Gabi didn't even think about chang-ing out of her dress as she put the children to bed, only realising she was still wearing it when Ana, almost asleep, thrust out her hand and patted the material on her arm and announced *'bonito'*. It was the highest compliment she could have received for a dress she had designed herself, she thought, backing out of the room and going to find Nate.

He was standing in front of the single floor-to-ceiling window that wrapped around half of the entire villa, looking out at the stunning nightscape on display. He had removed his tie and cufflinks, the sleeves of his shirt rolled back in such a carelessly attractive way it almost stung.

If Gabi could have slipped off to her own room and not seen him again she would have, coward that she was. But the one design flaw of her dress—one she promised herself to rectify—was that she couldn't get out of it without help.

He caught her gaze in the window's reflection and simply watched as she approached, waiting. She looked away, unable to hold his gaze. She knew she must have sounded utterly irrational and churlish, resenting such a gift from her *husband*—the word felt strange in her heart. But how could she explain? How could she find the words to tell him how much it hurt, wanting more than she was allowed to have?

'Can…?' She tried again after clearing her throat. 'Can you…?'

He turned. 'You need my help?' he asked.

Gabi nodded, startled when he let out a cynical laugh.

'Your dress? You need my help with your dress.' He nodded to himself as if angry.

Heat poured into her soul. 'Look, if you don't want to—'

He raised his hand, cutting her off. 'It's not about want, Gabi.'

'Nate,' she said, exhausted and done, 'I don't know what the subtext is here. I don't know why you're angry, when you changed all the plans that I knew, when you basically upended everything, just because you can—'

'I'm angry, Gabi, because you don't *let* me help.'

Gabi pulled herself up short and Nate shook his head as if in disbelief, as if realising she had absolutely no clue what he was talking about.

'You don't let me help with the children, you don't let me help *you*. I'm not allowed to make changes to your routine. I'm not allowed *in*.'

Shocked by the truth of his words, Gabi's own anger rose. 'I'm trying to navigate the convenient marriage you wanted and the parental role you need, Nate. It's not easy,' she snapped.

'There is nothing *convenient* about any of this.'

'On that, we can finally agree. I'll see you in the morning.' She turned, furious tears pressing against the backs of her eyes, determined to get to her room before he could see them fall.

'Your dress,' he called after her.

'I'll rip it if I have to,' she yelled, forcing aside the sob that filled her chest. She slipped quietly into the room next to the children's, hating the sight of the rose petals that she was sure Nate hadn't even seen, making a mockery of her wedding night. A bucket beside the bed held a bottle of champagne and melted ice water and she wanted to hurl it out of the window.

The tears came then. Silently, in the way she had

learned as a child. Hot and hurting as they poured down her cheeks. She snatched at the zip behind her, clumsy fingers suddenly uncaring of the dress that had brought her so much joy, and tore at the material desperately, needing to get it off her body.

Eventually, with only a little ripping, she wrangled the silk and lace from her skin and sobbed, sucking in a lungful of the first clear air she'd taken that day. She scrubbed her make-up from her face in the shower, where her tears were nearly invisible, and from habit waited until she was sure that they had run dry before getting out.

She slipped between the satin sheets, ignoring the rose petals, but as she finally closed her eyes and tried to find sleep, she couldn't stop hearing his words in her head.

'You don't let me help... I'm not allowed in.'

A tear escaped from beneath her closed eyes, because she realised she had never learned to trust that, if she asked, help would be given. And she couldn't help but think how terribly sad that was.

An hour later, Nate gently prised open her door to make sure that she was okay. He stayed in the doorway, unwilling to wake her, watching her sleeping amongst the red rose petals, for enough time for the moon to pass overhead before turning away.

Nate clutched his espresso in a death grip, knowing it was his only lifeline to staying awake at that moment. Last night had hardly been the typical wedding night, but, for a man who had never intended to marry, he wasn't that surprised. He'd not slept a wink, tossing and turning between memories of their kiss, the wedding, the single night they'd shared more than two years ago, and his words to her. Words that had fallen from his lips out of sheer frustration and his own tiredness. He should never had said them. He'd been hoping that Gabi would adjust, would slowly start to give him more space, more responsibility, but she hadn't. Instead, it had almost been getting worse.

At around three in the morning he'd begun to fear that she didn't trust him. That she didn't think she could leave the children with him. That because of his aneurism—a weakness, a vulnerability—he was unreliable. Wasn't that why he'd not told anyone outside the family about what had happened to him? Knowing that the business world would not only smell blood in the water but take advantage of it too. But to think that it made her doubt him as a parent...

'Morning.' Gabi ventured quietly from the doorway to the kitchen.

He turned, hating the way that, after searching her face, he could see signs of her distress last night too. He looked around her but couldn't see Ana or Antonio.

'They're still asleep, miraculously,' Gabi said, correctly interpreting his thoughts. 'Which is a good thing—' she sighed '—because I want to talk to you.'

Nate nodded, ready to accept whatever resolution she had come to, knowing that she had done so because of the way she carried herself. Determined, which he respected. Powerful, which he admired. Beautiful, which he couldn't deny.

She came into the room and sat at a gorgeous golden oak hand-carved table, warm from the gentle morning sun as it streamed through the windows. She looked like a summer fairy, Nate thought, before blaming the ridiculous thought on a considerable lack of sleep.

He took a seat opposite her and waited.

'I owe you an apology,' Gabi said, and he immediately shook his head in denial.

'No, you don't.'

She held his gaze. 'I do,' she said solemnly.

'Gabi—'

'Nate, *por Dios*, if you don't let me finish—'

'Sorry,' he said, raising his arms in surrender, biting back the urge to insist that she didn't.

She flexed her hands against the table. 'You were right,' she admitted. 'I didn't—*don't*—let you help. I can't. Because...' She took a breath. 'Because I grew up in a household where everything I had came with strings. Where if I was given something, it was either taken away later or used against me.'

The fury Nate felt towards Renata Casas increased with every word Gabi spoke.

'And where most of the time, when I asked for help, it was either dismissed or forgotten,' Gabi said, and Nate's heart pounded in his chest.

'When I couldn't get hold of you to tell you about the twins,' she said, and Nate felt a fresh twist of shame unfurl in his gut, 'I had to go to my brother. Javier, who had already been so damaged by our mother. I... I know that he would never say such a thing, let alone think it, but I was afraid that I and my children were a burden to him that he might eventually resent.'

Pink, painful-looking flushes appeared in patches beneath the gentle tan of Gabriella's skin. He had done that to her. His neglect had done that and he needed to know, needed to hear it all. Not as punishment, but so that he'd never forget what she had felt because of his inaction.

'That was terrible for me because I...' Gabi struggled to force the words through the hurt that had accumulated over the years. But Nate knew he deserved to hear the truth. The only way that they would be able to move forward, even remotely successfully co-parent, would be if she was completely honest with him. 'I didn't want to get used to his help, only to have it taken away.' His love. She hadn't wanted her brother to take away his love...like her parents had done. 'And then you came and... And signing a paper and wearing a ring doesn't suddenly make me feel as if you will stay, because my father didn't,' she said with a shrug, as if those words didn't beat against her fragile heart with the strength of a battering-ram. 'He didn't. He remarried and made himself another family. And my mother? Well, she's been married three times, so it's hardly something I see as reliable. And—'

Her words stopped when Nate reached across the table and placed his hands over where her fingers were picking at each other. Suddenly Gabi felt both impossibly young and terribly old, and, above all, utterly vulnerable.

'That will not happen here,' he vowed.

She tried to shake him off.

'Gabi, whatever happens, you will be taken care of, protected, financially at least.'

'It's not about finances.'

'No,' he admitted. 'It's not, but at least that is something that you can see on an account statement and know. The house is in your name. I have set up accounts for you and the children. I have no access to them. I cannot close them.'

His words did soothe something in her, but she also knew they were a patch, to cover her real need.

'As for parenting and supporting you? This is only something I can show you daily, until hopefully you don't have to question it any more. If you let me. If you *trust* me.'

Gabi wasn't deaf to the plea in his voice, nor the urging of her heart. She knew that she needed at least to let him try—let herself try.

'But Nate, you can't just make decisions that directly impact me and the children without me knowing. You've been in our lives for five minutes—'

He opened his mouth to speak but she knew what he was going to say. 'I know that's not your fault, but it is fact. And there are things you don't know about the children. What if they'd been terrified of the water and you didn't stop to ask? What if Antonio had nightmares sleeping away from his bed, or Ana had allergies?'

Nate stared at her, understanding swirling in his gaze, and at least had the grace to look a little ashamed.

'We need to be able to talk, Natē. Share things,' she concluded, 'before decisions are made.'

Like we promised in our vows, she thought.

He looked back up at her, sincerity shining in his eyes as if he'd heard her silent plea. 'Agreed.'

Eventually she nodded.

'Gabi, I need to tell you. Your mother—'

'Was there yesterday,' she said with a sad smile. 'I know.'

Nate frowned, clearly having believed that he'd kept it a secret. 'I didn't want it to spoil the day.'

Gabi let out a huff. 'I think we did that well enough ourselves, don't you?' she asked ruefully. But she could at least realise that he had tried, in his own way, to protect her.

'Do Ana and Antonio know about her—Renata?'

Gabi looked down at her hands and shook her head. 'I left her house the night you visited and have never been back. She never tried to reach me, and I didn't want to speak to her. I didn't see her again until court… And grandparents have never come up around them because…'

Because she and Javi had only ever referred to her as Renata, and because there had not been any other grandparents in their lives for them to ask about her mother. Because, as she knew, his parents had passed.

'Let's start again,' he said, slapping his hands on the table determinedly, but whether he was trying to avoid the topic of his parents or something else she couldn't tell. 'There are staff here, a chef and a housekeeper. Let's make the most of the next two weeks, to take it as easy as possible. Find a new routine for us and the children, with no stress or worries. Together, as a team.'

'A team?' Gabi tried the word out for size, beginning to allow herself to hope. To wonder what she could do

if she had more time, if she let other people in to help.
If she *trusted*. 'A team,' she repeated with a little more
determination.

And they did just that.

It wasn't easy, Nate discovered, working out how to
manage the twins together, especially when they were
already so quick to adapt and test the waters with them
each separately in order to get their own way. But it
brought Nate and Gabi closer much more quickly, forcing them to be a united front against the sheer might
of their children's strong and fascinating personalities.
Having someone else to cook and clean—things that he
now realised Gabi had done herself in order to lessen
the financial debt and burden she felt she owed Javier—
was an absolute godsend.

It gave them time to spend together as a family, but it
also gave Gabi less to do and within days he could see
how the dark circles he'd only just realised were there
were beginning to fade. They lounged around a shallow
children's pool, perfect and safe for Ana and Antonio,
who were proving to be utter water babies. They were
getting used to him now, and were beginning to interact
with him so much more. Ana had been hard won and
definitely the last holdout, but it had only made Nate
more determined to earn her trust. She took her cues
from her mother and was a lot more watchful than Gabi
realised, Nate thought.

In the evenings, after the twins had been put to bed,
dinner would be waiting for them out on the terrace,
where the heat of the day had gentled and the cover of

night brought the flowering scents of bougainvillea and the sound of cicadas.

And he didn't miss England one bit, Nate realised. All the while he'd been in Switzerland, recovering and rehabbing, he'd missed his desk, his sleek bachelor pad, with an almost obsessive fixation. But since coming to Spain, since meeting his children, since marrying Gabi…he'd not even thought of it once.

They quickly settled into the routine of sharing dinner, a glass of wine and anecdotes of their childhoods. Nate was determined to listen, and if Gabi noticed that he didn't quite share as much as she did then she didn't say anything. Slowly, day by day, he felt himself beginning to relax, only having to turn his attention to a few work-related matters for the duration of his honeymoon.

And when he had a spare moment he was beginning to consider whether it was sensible to liquidate his shares in Casas Textiles after all. Perhaps there was something there for Gabi? But only if Renata was utterly and completely removed. He thrust aside thoughts of his mother-in-law because when he did so he felt the pressing of a headache against his brain in a way that he neither liked nor wanted to know about.

Gabi laughed at a story she was telling, and once again he was struck by how incredibly beautiful she was. And she had absolutely no idea. Everything about her seemed connected in a way that was both natural and sensual at the same time. He'd seen her in her wedding dress, her bikini, her hair soaking, her skin damp and wrapped in a towel, and he'd had to retreat to his room before he embarrassed them both. So, while he should be celebrating his victories with her as a parent, he couldn't help but feel that he was utterly failing in his own attempts to keep this marriage out of the bedroom. Because in bed, alone, each night he dreamed only of her.

CHAPTER EIGHT

A WEEK AFTER returning from their honeymoon and Gabi was already missing the staff. Nate had made several offers to employ help, but Gabi was resistant. Resistant, reluctant and resentful. She'd been managing just fine by herself before he'd come along—shouldn't they need *less* help with an extra pair of hands? But somehow she was even more exhausted.

In truth, she didn't want strangers in her house. She didn't want people there to judge her if she got things wrong or made a mistake. She knew she was a good mother. She knew she was, but she couldn't help feeling that having help would be like admitting she couldn't cope.

Nate had flown to London that morning and promised to be back later that evening, and deep down she'd been looking forward to it, hoping that the reprieve from his presence would lessen the anxious yearning that had built since the wedding. She'd blamed the time spent by the pool on the honeymoon.

It was one thing seeing a man in his prime, broad shoulders, toned, *defined*, but seeing that same man play so lovingly and patiently with his children? It was a level of attraction she hadn't experienced before. A level of possession and ownership buried deep within the desire she felt for him, because that was her *husband*. And then she remembered his edict: convenient. Name only. Co-parenting. And seesawed back to miserable yearning again.

Gabi poured herself a glass of wine and sat down on the sofa, staring out at the night sky through the open French windows. She promised herself that she'd grab something more substantial than the bowl of peanuts she'd brought with her into the sitting room. She had a basket of washing still to fold, and had planned to make a start on sauce for the children's lunches, but she just needed five minutes to herself.

The scent of honeysuckle and bougainvillea slipped in on the breeze and it soothed her thoughts. Her mind finally settled enough to wander a little and, in her imagination, she saw wisps of material, the line of a dress, a vibrant colour from a flower that had caught her eye on the island where they'd honeymooned, the way the petals were layered, making her think of skirts and...

Her fingers reached for a pencil, wanting to get the images from her mind onto paper. It had been so long since inspiration had struck, her confidence cruelly decimated by her mother, her time utterly consumed by her children. She'd begun to fear that it might have gone. She might have lost it for ever, if she'd ever had it in the first place. But her wedding dress, the comments, Hope's praise, they'd given her a push in the secret part of her that still cherished the hope to make her dreams come true one day.

She debated for a moment. She really should get on to the housework. But the desire, the need, to channel this moment of creativity was so strong it wouldn't be denied. She grabbed a pen and some paper from beside the landline and gave herself five minutes. Just five and then she'd get back to the laundry.

Nate checked his watch as he put his key in the door and winced. It was nearly two in the morning. The meetings had run on and had left a strange tension in his neck that even now, rolling his shoulders, didn't quite shift. He didn't like it, and he didn't like what it made him feel, what it made him fear, so he pushed it down and shook it off.

At least he'd achieved what he'd set out to do, he thought as he put his briefcase down in the hallway and went to the kitchen to pour himself a whisky. Another thing he shouldn't be doing. He knew it was bad for him, the doctors had recommended a very healthy lifestyle to follow, but Nate clung to the glass as if it were his act of defiance, his proof that things were back to normal, the way that they had been *before*.

Which was why, despite the opportunity to sell one of his companies to a consortium based in Norway, he'd decided against it. He was managing just fine, no balls were being dropped, because he was better now. He didn't need to compromise his dreams for the future from *before*. That was why he'd spent so long in Switzerland after all. Making sure he was back to normal. Working at full capacity and—

He stopped in the doorway to the living room, finding Gabi asleep on the sofa. She was surrounded by bits of paper and a half-drunk glass of wine had been discarded next to a bowl with a handful of nuts still left in it. Was that all she'd had for dinner? He hadn't noticed any pots or pans in the sink, or the food she would often leave for him in the fridge.

Even from here he could see the dark smudges beneath her eyes were back. And he had to wrangle his frustration with the stubborn woman. She was working herself to the bone—had been ever since the twins had been born, he imagined. Why wouldn't she accept his help?

You know why.

Yes, her mother had been a monster, her father little better by his absence. But didn't Nate have some responsibility to bear? He'd promised to show her that she could trust him to help, and had he? Had he really?

He frowned, putting the glass of whisky down and making his way towards the sofa. He picked up one of the pieces of paper left on the coffee table beside the wine and stared. He might not be a fashionista, but he had grown up in an international department store, specialising in luxury items from household to fashion and everything in between. He didn't have his sister's eye, nor his mother's, but he knew what would sell, and as he stared at the dress design on the page he knew it was good. Not just good, but *really* good.

He picked up a few more pieces of paper. He could tell the early ones had begun with less confidence, a little less daring. But, as she had gone on, the lines became firmer, stronger, more determined. At some point she must have grabbed coloured pens from the children's box, but even then she'd tempered and blended the garish primary colours into splashes and lines of colour that gave just enough of an idea of what it could look like.

Without thinking, with his phone he snapped a few pictures of some of the stronger designs and sent them to his sister with 'What do you think?' as a message. It was a running joke between them, because most of the time they knew exactly what the other would think.

He perched down on the edge of the sofa beside Gabi's feet and sighed. She was running herself ragged, leaving not even a minute for herself, and it had to stop. Tomorrow, he would fix it, but tonight he needed to get her off the sofa and into her room.

Unwilling to wake her, even for that short walk, he stood and scooped her up into his arms. And, just like that, the world shifted. She settled against his chest, her hand coming up to press near to a heart that leapt beneath her touch. The subtle floral perfume that he associated only with her rose to tease his senses. The way her body pressed against his sent him straight back to the night they'd shared in Madrid...and memories of what they'd shared, the delicious, heady pleasure that had made him half sure he'd fallen in love before he'd felt absolutely sure he'd been betrayed. So much confusion and so much emotion around that night, but even now he still felt a magnetic pull to her. To be with her.

But things were so new and precarious between them, he couldn't risk giving in to his base desires. Forcing his body's wayward reaction back under control, he walked towards her room, pausing only to briefly look in on the children as they passed. He pushed the door to her bedroom open as Gabi's hand reached up from his chest to curl around his neck, gently grasping the hair at his nape. His pulse picked up, the accidentally sensual contact tearing at the fine thread of his control. Despite the gentle breeze through the open window, here in her bedroom, the scent of her, the sense of Gabi, was so much stronger.

He walked to her bed and carefully laid her down, needing to retreat before he did something unconscionable. But as he began to pull away, the hand around his neck tightened and he looked down to find Gabi staring up at him, eyes open, awake and full of the same yearning he felt deep in his bones. Heat poured over his skin, settling into every atom and fibre of his being.

Gabi's skin flushed, her eyes sparked and her mouth opened as if to say something and he wouldn't, couldn't, hear it. Coward that he was, he gently removed her hand from his neck and backed away from Gabi's bed, unable to turn away from the longing in her gaze until he reached the corridor and closed the door behind him.

It wouldn't have taken much for Gabi to convince herself that what had happened last night had been a dream. It had that kind of quality in her mind. But she knew herself well and if it had been a dream, Nate wouldn't have left her. So, embarrassed and a little confused and very tired, she dragged herself out of bed and into the shower, before heading to the twins' room.

But their beds were empty. She knew that they were okay, realised in an instant that they were probably with

Nate, but adrenaline was a sharp painful spike through her chest as she hurried towards the kitchen.

There she found Antonio staring up at Nate with banana and soggy wheat all over his face, clapping furiously as Ana tried to put her feet on Nate's shoulders as he held her above him, laughing.

'Ana, *basta*!' he teased. 'I'm not a climbing frame,' he said, his voice different to what she'd heard before, gentler. 'No, you can't do it!' he gently mocked.

'Yes, Papá, yes, Ana do it!' she said, clearly enough for them to understand.

Nate froze—just a moment, not enough for Ana to notice, but Gabi caught it, caught the way his entire being resonated with some indefinable emotion, because she'd known it too, the first time her children had called her Mamá. In that instant he caught sight of Gabi in the doorway, his eyes so full of parental love, the utter intensity of it, that she couldn't help but smile and nod, understanding that he needed to know that she'd heard it too.

'Ana, Ana, Ana,' he cried, dropping her down into his arms, sneaking kisses on her belly and making her scream with laughter. Antonio looked between Nate and her, cheering and not seeming to feel even remotely left out, but enjoying his sister's happiness.

Gabi pressed a hand against the swelling of her heart, knowing that, no matter what attraction she felt for Nate, she wouldn't dare risk *this*, their family, for something as dangerous or selfish as her wants. So when she looked back at Nate she told herself that last night *had* been a dream, and forced whatever feelings that remained so deep she would hopefully forget them.

* * *

By the time Gabi returned from putting the twins down for their late-morning nap, Nate had a coffee waiting for her on the garden table. She eyed it warily and Nate realised that this had become their 'discussion' routine whenever they had something they needed to talk to the other about.

'What is it? I've got to get lunch ready.'

'It's about that, actually,' Nate said, sitting down to show that he wasn't going anywhere. She eyed him suspiciously, but he gestured to the seat opposite him.

'It's time.'

'What's time?'

'It's time that we hired some help,' he said, trying not to roll the tension out of his shoulders.

'We don't need it, Nate. We're perfectly fine—'

'You're exhausted,' he said quietly, aware of the precarious line he was treading. She'd told him enough about her mother, about her need to give their children the opposite of what she'd had, that he knew how delicate this needed to be. 'I'm tired just looking at all you do around here. I'm helping, I know, and you're letting me, but…wouldn't it be easier, better, if you had more dedicated time to focus on the twins?'

The moment the words came out of his mouth, he knew they had struck wrong and he tried not to wince at the shiver of hurt that cut through her gaze.

'Are you implying that I don't give them enough attention?' she demanded, her accent getting a little thicker with the strength of her emotion.

'No!' he cried. 'I'm not. I'm *really* not. I know how

much you do for them, how much you give them and...'
he tried to choose his words carefully '...and I think it
might be too much.'

She frowned and he used her moment of confusion
to push on. 'You're exhausted,' he said again. 'But the
thing is, you don't have to be. We can have a housekeeper, someone to help with the cooking and cleaning.
And we can have someone to help with the children.
There are two of them, Gabi. Twins, and I know from
personal experience just how draining we can be. You
need a minimum of two pairs of hands just to keep them
breathing half the time. But that's them. This is about
you. Don't you want more than just being a mother?' he
asked, thinking of the inspiration he'd seen in her drawings. Hating the fact that he hadn't known that she'd designed her wedding dress until he'd spoken to his sister
late last night. 'You are an excellent mother,' he stressed.
'Don't you think having a little time for yourself will
only make that even better?' he probed.

'Nate, if you can't handle them—'

'This isn't about me, and I *can* handle them,' he
growled, frustration tipping the tension towards a headache and getting the better of him. 'This is about making sure that the mother of my children doesn't break
herself by exhausting herself needlessly and sacrificing
her own wants and needs.'

Gabi pulled back from the table as if she'd been
slapped and half of him wished he could take back the
words while the other half knew they needed to be said.

'I know I've only been here for a few months now,
Gabi, but I can already tell that this is a marathon, not

a sprint, and that we should take all the help we can get in order to make sure that the time we spend with our children is as easy and carefree as possible. I also know that the time we spend as individuals rather than as parents is just as important,' he said, pulling her design from last night from his pocket, unfolding it and passing it to her across the table.

'You owe it to yourself as much as those children to follow your dreams, Gabi. Having help means that you can. And the way the children are growing and learning, it's even just basic safety to have someone to help *and* it's good socialisation,' he said, knowing that he sounded like the parenting books he pored over in secret whenever he got the chance. He felt like a bastard, but he knew that using the twins' safety and benefit would win her over far more easily and quickly than for her own sake.

'Can I think about it?' she asked, and he nodded, getting the sense that he might have finally swayed her towards the idea.

Gabi had warred with the decision, even though she'd known he was right. She'd forced herself to push past her own fears to see that it was best for her children. Their children. So she agreed to hire not only a housekeeper but someone to help with the children, knowing that it made the most sense. But the person she chose surprised everyone, most especially Nate. And Gabi decided to enjoy every minute of it.

'I'm not sure about this,' Nate said, closing the door on her favourite applicant.

They had been interviewing for two days and she knew that it had tested his patience. She had rejected the English nanny because no one could convince Gabi that the woman knew how to smile. Nate had vetoed Anna-Marie, the eccentric woman from Órgiva, when she'd told him off for drinking coffee. Names and faces had passed through the two days of interviews, all of whom had been *fine* but not good. Until now.

'Bilingual in Spanish and English, a degree in child education, *five* years' experience, with first class references. What is there to complain about? Unless you're being sexist.'

'I am *not* sexist.' Nate's quick and outraged retort made her hide a smile.

'Wonderful. Because he's starting next week.'

Gabi had to turn away before she laughed at the sight of the flickering muscle at his jaw. Oddly, she'd known there wasn't any true heat to his objection, she could feel it. Just as she could feel that Jorge would fit in perfectly. The twins had loved him on sight, and she'd been touched by how his entire focus revolved around them as soon as they came into the room. Children noticed things like that. She had as a child.

Jorge had asked what *her* concerns were about the process. He'd been the only one, as if he had the emotional sense or intelligence to see that this was hard for her. She also knew that he'd impressed Nate, despite his grumbling, and was looking forward to when he moved in.

The villa's small pool house at the back of the estate was perfect for him. He'd explained that his parents lived close by and that was why he'd wanted to stay in the area, which demonstrated how perfect he was to help her care for her twins. From the moment he arrived, Jorge fitted in to their days seamlessly, having fun with the new housekeeper who, despite being nearly thirty years older than him, he flirted with shamelessly.

The change for her was almost instantaneous. Not in the typical structure of the day; mornings and breakfast remained her and Nate's responsibility, at her request, as was putting them to bed. But it was during the day that she realised she had more time. Not having to cook, the laundry and cleaning being done for her. She oscillated between feeling guilty and a huge sense of relief. She'd pick up a book to read, just because she *could*. But still her old sketches and pens and pencils, all her university work, waited untouched in the study she'd claimed as her own. As if she wasn't quite sure that she'd earned it yet.

But it was about two weeks after Jorge started that she began to realise how much Nate had been juggling too. A little less tension showed around his shoulders, a tiredness she could only identify now that it was not there in the shadows beneath his eyes. He started taking some meetings in his office during the day.

'Are they asking more from you now?' she'd asked out of curiosity once as he'd headed towards another meeting.

He'd looked blankly at her, then frowned. 'No?'

'It's just that you seem to have a lot of meetings.'

He blinked. 'I can take them during the day now.'

This time *she'd* frowned, only realising what that meant as he'd shrugged and left the room. He'd been spending his days with them and while she'd been sleeping he'd been running several empires. Guilt pricked painfully at her conscience.

She had been relying on herself for so long that she'd started *thinking* only of herself. Or perhaps it had just been survival mode, doing what needed to be done. But she couldn't let that happen again because they were a team.

She was letting herself enjoy the evenings they spent together too, as their conversations developed from discussing the children to hopes for the future, things that made them laugh, experiences that either differed from each others' so greatly they were fascinating, or were so similar it was startling.

An ease began between them, creeping slowly closer to something more. Touches were so fleeting she thought she might be imagining them. Eyes lingering just a little longer than necessary. A heat simmering gently beneath their interactions, something so vastly different from the incendiary night they'd shared so long ago that it took Gabi a while to realise it was there. She tried to ignore it, to push it away. Because for the first time in so very long she was happy, she realised. Genuinely happy. Her children were the joy of her heart, but Nate was providing a peace and a stability she'd never known. And she felt a tentative trust in him beginning to form.

She was looking out at the sunlight dancing off the pool in the garden when her watch alarm pinged to let her know to wake up the twins. She gently pushed open their door and peeked in. Ana was standing up in her cot, her eyes glistening and cheeks pink.

'Qué tienes, mi amor?'

Ana pointed at Antonio. Gabi turned and leaned into his cot, gently rubbing Antonio's belly.

'Antonio,' she whispered, but he barely lifted his eyes. Concern snapped through her like lightning, but she forced herself to be gentle. 'Antonio,' she said, louder, trying to rouse him. She felt his forehead and it was burning up. Beneath her hand, his stomach felt almost solid.

'Nate!' she yelled. 'Nate!'

She picked Antonio up gently, feeling horror almost incapacitate her.

Nate rushed into the room, his words dying on his lips as he took in the sight of her, terrified and clutching their child to her chest.

'I don't know what's wrong...' She looked up at him helplessly. 'I need you. I don't know what to do,' she whispered.

'What do you want to do?' he asked, as if he trusted her completely.

'I want to go to the hospital.'

'Then we go to the hospital.'

CHAPTER NINE

NATE'S HEART SEEMED to stop beating and he wasn't sure if it was ever going to start again. Gabi passed Antonio to him and picked up Ana. In the background he heard Jorge run into the living area as the housekeeper yelled and cried.

Ignoring them all, he rushed out to the car, cradling his son, and when he turned Gabi was by his side. Just over his shoulder he saw Jorge now with Ana, and Gabi told him they'd follow. He gave Antonio back to Gabi and opened the door for her, before rushing round to the driver's side.

'Forget the car seat,' he told her before she could even ask. 'We don't have time.'

Nate drove as fast as he could, not caring about laws or speed limits, only safety, only his child.

He called his assistant from the car's hands-free system.

'Mike, I need you to call the nearest hospital and tell them that I'm bringing in a barely conscious twenty-month-old child with a fever and a firm abdomen. Tell them I want their top paediatric consultant to meet us in the emergency room. When that's done, call Dr Brunner and tell him to call me. If he can't get through, just tell him to keep trying until I answer.'

He barely heard his assistant respond before hanging up the call as he overtook a truck winding too slowly around the turns in the road.

'Sorry,' he said to Gabi, impossibly conscious of every jolt or movement to her and their precious cargo.

'I don't care,' she said, her lips resting on the super-fine hair on Antonio's head. 'Do whatever you have to,' she commanded, and he hit the accelerator.

His neck ached from flicking his gaze from the road to the seat beside him, unable to stop himself from covering the hand Gabi had wrapped protectively around Antonio with his own, in between changing gear.

Nate counted down each painful, worrying minute until they pulled into the emergency room, abandoning the car in a doctors' parking space and running around to open the door for Gabi, while shouting for help.

He felt his phone vibrate where he'd shoved it into his top pocket, but ignored it as several staff members dressed either in scrubs or white coats came running.

Gabi hurled Spanish back and forth with the staff so quickly that all he could do was make space for the gurney they brought to them. Gabi looked up at him, torn between needing to share the information and wanting to translate for him, but he shook his head. 'Do what you have to.'

She nodded once and continued her conversation with who Nate had decided was the lead doctor. He stood back and looked down at his son's small body as people crowded around him, hooking up monitors and trying to flash a light in his eyes.

His chest ached as if someone had cleaved it in two and he didn't care that tears pressed against the backs of his eyes. His attention snapped to the entrance when he heard Jorge calling his name loudly and clearly above all the commotion. He turned and beckoned the young man, who looked both competent and scared for them at the same time.

Without a word, Nate opened his arms for Ana, who was crying and saying 'Papá!' over and over again. He held his daughter to his heart and tried to soothe her even though it felt as if the world was coming apart at his feet.

His phone buzzed again and he held Ana, kept his eyes glued to Antonio and Gabi and answered his phone.

'Nathanial.'

'Dr Brunner.'

'Where are you?'

'The hospital in Nerja, southern Spain.'

'Okay. Hold on.'

Nate heard muffled voices and tapping on a keyboard, thankful that the no-nonsense physician who had overseen his medical treatment was ruthlessly efficient and knew him well enough to understand what he needed.

'Your son is twenty months old, with a fever, abdominal stiffness and lethargy.'

'Yes.'

'Okay. The hospital you're in has an excellent reputation. Well-trained staff and no red flags.'

'But?' Nate demanded, sensing the other man's professional hesitation.

'I still want to send my colleague down to you. I trained with him and I'd have him care for my children if I had them.'

'Done.'

'Okay. I would, in no other circumstances, speculate with such limited information, but I want you to first know that this is not presenting as an aneurism—as I'm sure that's where your mind is going right now.'

Nate wanted to drop to his knees and weep. It was such a shocking sensation, he hardly noticed that Jorge pressed him into a chair beside the bed where they were assessing Antonio.

'It is probable that this is a UTI—a urinary tract infection—but I would like to speak to the physician when he has a moment to confirm his thoughts. I'm fluent in Spanish so the language won't be a problem. Do you have someone you can pass the phone to, until that happens?'

'Yes,' Nate said, clearing his throat, his mind half full of words of thanks, but mostly still full of fear.

'Go be a dad, let me be a doctor. I'll stay on the line until I speak to the treating physician and then I'll speak to you again and tell you what I know.'

Nate turned to Jorge, told him what Dr Brunner had asked, and entrusted the phone and the task to the young man and turned back to watching Gabi nodding and shaking her head, answering the multitude of questions the medics had for her.

Knowing that she was doing everything in her power

to get Antonio the right treatment, Nate fixed his gaze on his son and willed him to be okay.

Shortly after they had been admitted, they were moved to a private room on a floor higher up in the building. It was spacious with a sofa where Gabi, Nate and Ana were huddled together and a chair that was alternately occupied by the housekeeper and Jorge.

At some point the head of paediatrics had come in with another doctor and spoken to both of them, along with a translator provided by the hospital so that they could both understand and so that Gabi didn't have to do it herself. Before they'd left, the doctors had asked for a word with Nate and Gabi had barely noticed, returning to her vigil beside Antonio. Jorge had offered to take Ana home if they'd wanted, but neither she nor Nate had wanted to be away from either of their children for even a moment.

By the time that she had been reassured that her son was in neither a critical condition nor likely to get worse, she checked her phone and saw the seventeen missed calls from her brother. Nate had encouraged her to call him back. She knew without a shadow of a doubt that Javier and Emily would be here in a heartbeat if they could, but they were currently in Sri Lanka.

It took nearly twenty minutes to convince them that there was no point coming back to Spain, and she was able to say with absolute conviction that she had all the support she needed in Nate. He'd been a rock, completely and utterly. And it was only when she put the phone back in her bag that she realised that he was still holding her free hand. It had been that way, off and on, for both of them since arriving at the hospital. A near constant need to touch, to know, to reassure and to seek assurance. Giving and taking passing between them like the ebb and flow of a tide, when needed and when able to provide.

She'd asked him if he wanted to call Hope, but Nate shook his head and explained that he'd wait until he knew they were home safely, not wanting to worry her. Gabi wanted to point out that that wasn't the reason to call his sister. It wasn't about sharing information, it was about sharing the burden, but she could see he would not welcome such advice, certainly not now.

Ana was asleep on his chest, tears clumping her long lashes together and still red-cheeked, but soothed enough to sleep. Antonio was hooked up to an IV bag of antibiotics and monitors since the tests had come back and confirmed that he was suffering from a UTI. Nate had accepted the information with a grim nod and returned his focus to his son.

When Gabi had fretted that she'd done something wrong, that she should have seen it earlier, that she could have done something to prevent it, Nate had pulled her into his side and gently shushed her with reassurances. She had gone to him, used him, relied on him and he had been her strength. No, he hadn't taken away her fear, but he had weathered it with her, been there to lean on, to reassure her, to care for her. As he had promised to do on their wedding day.

She must have fallen asleep on Nate, because his arm was around her, gently waking her. 'Gabi, he's up.'

It took only seconds for her to regain her senses and spring to his side, but there he was, her son, a little red-cheeked and seemingly utterly furious with the IV fluids.

'The antibiotics work quickly with infections like these,' said a nurse, smiling. 'You should be able to take him home in a few hours.'

The relief Gabi felt was near euphoric. She looked to Nate beside her and saw exactly the same thing reflected in his gaze, felt the sudden and intense need to kiss him, to have that closeness with him, to draw that energy from him, but wavered. As if he'd sensed her thoughts, he pulled her gently to him and pressed his lips to the top of her head. She told herself it was enough. It had to be.

Three hours later, the housekeeper threw open the door for them and welcomed them home. Gabi was bone-deep tired and reluctant to let either Ana or Antonio out of her sight. But even she could see that she needed to let them sleep and standing in the doorway and watching them wouldn't help anyone.

Jorge had offered to stay in the room, just in case, and even Nate had been touched by the offer, but he was happy that the monitor was enough. He sent Jorge off to the pool house to get some much-needed rest and thanked the housekeeper for making dinner before she left for the night, sniffing and cooing about how happy she was that the little ones were home safe.

Gabi watched in awe as Nate handled everyone with perfect calm and patience, leading her out to their table beneath the bougainvillea, where neither he nor she seemed to have any appetite for the food their house-keeper had lovingly and carefully provided.

'You were amazing today,' she admitted, falling back against the chair with exhaustion.

'Me?' he scoffed. 'You were the one who talked to all the doctors, told them that they needed to diagnose Antonio and quickly. Christ, Gabi. You were incredible.'

She felt a blush rise to her cheeks. 'I couldn't have done it without you. I was terrified.'

'So was I,' he admitted.

'Really? You just seemed so in control.'

He huffed out a bitter laugh. 'I thought my world was ending.' He put a hand to his chest as if even now his heart needed soothing.

It struck her then that it hadn't been that long since he'd been in hospital himself. And she hesitated to ask, but then realised she wanted to know. Needed to know.

'Did it bring back bad memories for you?' she asked.

Nate looked at her, the gentle dusk falling around them a time for sharing intimacies and secrets. 'It brought back bad fears perhaps, rather than memories. I thought...' He seemed to waver. 'I thought that it might have been an aneurism, like mine.'

'Oh, Nate,' she cried, reaching for his hand across the table. 'I didn't even think,' she said, horrified that it hadn't crossed her mind.

He shook his head. 'My doctor told me that it was incredibly unlikely, but I spoke to the paediatric consultant at the hospital, who agreed that when things settle down we should think about getting both Ana and Antonio in for a scan, just in case.'

'Why wait?' she asked, not sure why they would.

'The diagnostic tests aren't pleasant, and they're young, it could be scary. But I agree, we need to know, just in case. If that's okay with you.' Nate deferred to her, knowing that he wouldn't do anything without her agreement.

Gabi nodded quickly and determinedly, but the clouds were still in her gaze. 'Still, that must have made this entire thing so much worse for you.'

Nate shrugged, trying to dismiss it, but he couldn't shake the image of Antonio limp in her arms. He'd genuinely thought for a moment that he might lose his son and feared it might have actually broken something in him.

He didn't talk about his feelings, he wasn't used to or even comfortable with sharing such things, but Gabi had been vulnerable with him. She had trusted him. Perhaps it was time for him to do the same.

'I hate hospitals. I *hate* them,' he said, surprising himself with the vehemence in his voice. 'The smell, the noise, the hushed whispers of considerate nursing staff and the brash booming voices of consultants whose jobs are so important they don't care who hears them. But it's the patients. It's quiet in some and loud and selfish in others, but it's all the same. Desperation. Regret,' he said with a shrug, as if he hadn't felt those things himself.

'Yes, there are successes, yes, there is hope and there are miracles performed almost daily, everything—from someone learning to breathe on their own to the all-clear from cancer. Bloody miracles, like me—being able to live again, despite a damn bomb going off in my head,' he said bitterly, knowing that he probably sounded like a madman, angry and ungrateful.

'But all those people, all those miracles, they don't really prepare you for the fact that your life has completely and utterly changed. It will never be the same. You might get used to it for a while, a new pattern, a new routine, cut out meat and dairy, stop drinking alcohol, get regular exercise, the pain will go eventually and you'll get used to it.'

The words were pouring out of him, from where he couldn't tell, otherwise he'd stop them. Because he couldn't see Gabi any more, he could only see a montage of the two years of his life following his collapse. 'People watching and assessing in case you have a relapse, in case you show symptoms of another aneurism, or my sister asking me questions that test my memory, as if she was making sure it wasn't damaged. My grandfather watching me as if I might still ruin his empire one day,' he said, gripping the edge of the table with white-knuckled fingers.

He barely registered that Gabi had come to sit beside him, but he felt her presence like a balm, pushing back some of the anger at the depth of his hurt.

'And me. Not knowing if and when it might happen again, despite the quarterly scans and check-ups. Doubting myself, wondering what if…'

'Did you ever speak to Hope about it?'

Nate shook his head.

'*We aren't weak, Nathanial. We don't have that luxury.* The first time my grandfather said that to me was minutes before my parents' funeral. And within two

days my sister and I were shipped off to separate boarding schools,' he said, shaking his head. 'I always sus-
pected that he'd done that on purpose. To toughen us up.
The Harcourt version of "big boys don't cry".'

And while he knew that the Swiss centre's counsellor
had tried to help him see how damaging that had been,
it hadn't really registered until now, how that mentality
of silence, of doing it alone, had cut him off from the
support network that Gabi had managed to tentatively
build around her in her brother and sister-in-law.

His entire life, from the age of twelve onwards, had
been founded on the belief that you couldn't talk about
your feelings, you couldn't show emotion, that if you
hurt you hid it, learning only how to be a broken man.
Wasn't he still that?

'Some people,' he said, clearing the emotion from
his throat, 'when they recover from something like this,
become daredevils, tempting fate and death, having escaped it once. Others seem to double down on who and
what they were before.'

'And you?'

'Me? I don't know. I just don't know,' he admitted.

She reached out and gently loosened his fingers from
their grip on the table, threading her own through his,
her palm gently pressing against the back of his hand,
smaller, but somehow so much stronger.

'Your life changed in a single moment and nothing
you knew would be the same again. And now you are
putting one step in front of the other and looking for the
right path to take,' she said.

He looked at her beneath the veil of darkness, the

understanding in her eyes shining brighter than the night sky. 'Like you did? When you found out about the twins?' he realised.

She smiled. It wobbled a little, but it was there. 'Yes,' she admitted. 'Nothing stays the same, Nate.'

Her words were quiet in the unsettled air between them, and she wondered whether they sounded as prophetic to him as they did to her. She wished, so much, that things could have been different for him as a child. It sounded brutally cold and emotionally desolate. She hurt for him the same way that she'd hurt for herself—a soul-deep ache that only love could heal. But that kind of love took years to develop, she believed.

She inhaled deeply, letting the night air revive her, tuning in to the sounds and feel of it wrapping around her, suddenly aware of just how physically close she was to Nate, the heat of his body radiating out to dull the nip of cold on the gentle breeze.

She shivered, not from the drop in temperature but from awareness.

All those touches, throughout the day, earlier and now, they had slowly layered one over the other until she couldn't deny it. If she hadn't thought Nate was aware of it too, wanted it too, then she wouldn't have dared. But she felt it, that same heady intoxication that had urged her to follow him that night in the hotel, when she'd been so innocent and naïve. And yet, even now, knowing everything that would happen, and not just because of her babies, she would make the same decision all over again.

Because something connected her to this man, something primal, instinctive, otherworldly. Some part of her soul recognised him as if they had lived these lives before and would do so again.

The silence that built between them was steady but not uncomfortable. It was *expectant*. He gazed at her with such longing that it pulled at her pulse like the moon pulled the tide, drawing her to him with an unstoppable force that she couldn't fight, even if she'd wanted to.

Goosebumps scattered across her skin from where his thumb rubbed over the back of her hand. Such an innocent, simple touch, but one that had a seismic impact. Because he'd done it that night too. He'd laughed at himself and accused her of making him horny. She hadn't understood what he'd meant by that word, and had later looked it up to understand.

She'd been nervous when she'd got to his room, and he'd taken her onto the balcony and they'd talked beneath the stars, just like they had been doing the last few months, she realised with a sudden jolt. He'd eased her nerves and removed any kind of pressure. She'd told him she was leaving and he'd walked her to the door. He'd looked at her as if she were the world that he'd wait for, and that was why, instead of leaving that night, she'd turned into his arms and kissed him. She'd chosen to stay, not because she'd had a drink, not because her desires and herself were out of control, but because she'd known *him*.

'The last couple of years have changed us both, I think,' she said, finding the right words as she slowly stood from the seat, not quite letting go of his hand yet. 'And we aren't the same people we were that night.'

He looked up at her from the chair, his body seemingly relaxed, but she knew. She could see the line of tension that ran through his body, the sudden alertness, the watchfulness, a predator restrained only because he chose to be.

'This would change things again,' Nate warned.

'Everything changes all the time,' she informed him gently.

'But I need this not to change things,' he said, quietly but steadily. 'There's been too much—'

'Okay.'

'Okay?' he asked, as if trying to clarify what she wanted.

Gabi's lips curved into a sad smile in the darkness. She understood why he needed that sense of control, could see that he was trying to give her what he could. And for tonight, for now, that would be enough. Because she needed him. She needed something hot and passionate and real to surround her.

Antonio's illness had made her feel so cold, almost numb, and it had terrified her. So she was using Nate to make that disappear, to make her feel something again. Because when he touched her she felt *alive*, she felt beautiful and wanted and honoured, and tonight, of all nights, she needed those things.

'Take me to bed?' she asked and waited, breath held, to see what he would do. Seconds ticked by, minutes maybe, and she was about to give up...when he moved.

He leaned forward from the chair, not once taking

his eyes from her, slowly, smoothly, bringing himself to his full height so that she had to crane her neck just to keep that connection.

He stared at her as if memorising this moment, as if half afraid that it might never happen again. Or was that her? she wondered. She gazed up at him, his broad shoulders filling out the white shirt that glowed in the moonlight, open at the chest so that she could see the dusting of hair that had delighted her that night.

Clouds shifted across the moon, his face a study in chiaroscuro as he closed the distance between them with a step. But it was when the clouds finally passed across the night sky that she saw what was in his gaze and her heart snapped.

In his eyes she saw nothing but raw hunger.

CHAPTER TEN

'TAKE ME TO BED?'

Gabi's question roared through his veins, hurtling at a speed that navigated his body in the space of a heartbeat. Longing. He felt it in every inch of his being. He had done all that he could to keep his distance from her. He'd stepped back at every moment he could have stepped forward, refusing to trespass over the line he'd drawn between them. But now Gabi was asking him to and he didn't have the strength to deny her.

She looked up at him, her dark hair streaming down her back in gentle curls, her eyes glowing like labradorite in the moonlight with a desire that was different to what they'd shared in the hotel.

Then it had been nervous, excited, *illicit*. At the time he'd thought it just spending the night with a stranger, but now he knew the real risk that she had taken that night and somehow that made it more precious to him.

He shoved thoughts of the past away. Gabi was right. They had changed, but he told himself that what they *had* didn't have to. It *could* stay the same, if he willed it so. Because he couldn't lose them.

He couldn't. He'd only just found them. His *family*.

Strangely, that didn't chasten his desire for Gabi, but increased it. *Mine*, he realised. A possessive passion caught fire, immolating him where he stood. He breathed through the flames, relishing the burn as he swallowed, knowing that Gabi was the only balm that could soothe him now. Because it was a fire that came from her.

Now, when he looked at her, there were no nerves, no hesitation, just raw desire and a hunger that matched his own.

She swayed towards him at the same time as he leaned towards her, his hands already moving—one to cup her neck beneath the waterfall of her hair, the other cradling her cheek, not so that he could angle her face to meet him, but just so that he could get his damn hands on her.

Home.

When his lips met hers his entire being both relaxed and tensed, an exquisite torque that spun his heart and his head in different directions. She opened her mouth to his on a sigh and he took full advantage, finally slipping the leash of his restraint.

More.

He wanted more. To feel more, to touch more, to taste more. He walked them backwards without breaking the kiss, not with a destination in mind but a need. A need to feel her pressed beneath his body—and the bedroom was too bloody far away.

She came to an abrupt stop as her back hit the French window lightly, the gentle glow of illumination from the living room outlining her with a halo of gold. There was no fear in her eyes, just that same spark of more. A dare, a challenge.

Show me what you've got, her eyes were saying.

Please, the whimper that fell into his mouth begged.

He let his hands trace her body, caress her curves, fist the skirts of the dress she'd changed into when they'd got back from the hospital. Memories from earlier clouded his gaze, but Gabi cupped his jaw and pulled his gaze back to hers.

'Stay with me. Stay here,' she commanded like a goddess he wanted to worship.

He nodded, placed a carnal kiss to her lips, his tongue prising her mouth open and plundering all she had within. His heart raced, pounding as if trying to escape his chest, his fingers flexed against her hips as he pulled her against his powerful erection. She gasped again and it felt like a craving on his tongue.

He reluctantly pulled back from the kiss, not because he wanted to, but because there was something he wanted more. His lips curved into a smile as he saw the momentary disappointment in her eyes until he pressed open-mouthed kisses down the centre of her chest, his hands unable to resist the lure of her breasts, the perfect fit against his palms. His thumbs flicked over taut nipples and her body came alive beneath his, writhing with as of yet unsatisfied arousal.

He dropped to his knees as his hands reached her thighs, and his fingers ruched the material of her dress. Gabi's legs quivered and he heard the back of her head thunk gently against the glass. The thought of her naked and pressed up against that glass fired such an intense burst of need through his body that he missed a breath.

He looked up at her, meeting her gaze. She was biting her lip in a way that only increased his need for her.

'May I?' he asked, feeling the thrill of wicked desire catch light and the sparks in her eyes respond.

She nodded, a smile curving her lip from beneath the teeth that had it pinned. 'You may.'

That was all the permission he needed as he pulled her panties down her hips, thighs and one foot after the other, before placing them in his trouser pocket. His thumbs massaged her hips, soothing the quivering juncture, and he inhaled slowly and deeply, wanting to know this moment for ever. He parted her restless legs gently, her folds carefully, but, unable to resist any longer, he pressed his mouth to her in the most intimate of kisses.

The moan of pleasure that Gabi made was the most erotic thing he'd ever heard in his life. He swept his tongue across wet heat, unable to stop himself from pressing his mouth deeper against her, his thumb teasing her entrance as he sucked at first gently, then more firmly, on her clitoris, drawing—as he'd wanted—gasps and pleas from her. The sound of her begging thrilled him, not because she was surrendering to him but because she had surrendered to her own pleasure.

He felt it come for her, the power of it thrilling him nearly as much as her, as she trembled and writhed and bucked beneath his mouth and hands, her moans utterly mindless now as she reached higher and higher, a peak that eluded her again and again until finally it found her.

* * *

Nate was her sexual awakening and her sexual undoing. All the seams and ties and stitches that had held her together since he was last with her flew apart, leaving her open and exposed to his every touch. It took for ever to gather the scattered pieces of herself back together again, her body pulsing to a rhythm that she had barely learned once, but remembered and had missed so very much.

She shivered, not from the cold but by the shocking sensitivity he had wrought from her, her legs trembling until Nate rose from the floor and swept her up in his arms, encasing her in a warmth and protection that made her feel safer than she had ever felt before in her life. Unconsciously, her hand rested against his heart, searching for the strong, powerful beat that soothed her own.

Quietly, they passed the twins' room and he wavered, as if unsure whether to take her to his room or hers. She reached to pull him into a kiss, easing the momentary confusion in his eyes and reigniting a hunger that hadn't yet been satiated for him. He shouldered her door open, closed it behind him with a gentle press of his heel, before crossing to the bed and laying her gently down.

He stood back, staring at her long and deep.

'You are so beautiful,' he whispered as if conscious of the sleeping twins across the hall.

His words warmed her cheeks, but it was his care for the twins that made her want him more. From the bed, she held out her hand and when he took it she pulled him down against her body, welcoming him with a kiss that was already on her lips.

Yes, she was still reeling from an orgasm so intense it was still humming through her body, but it hadn't soothed the craving for *him*. The need to feel *him*, deep within her. The need to know whether she had imagined how it had felt to be so deeply connected to him. Her legs shifted against his and she realised that they were still clothed.

She started tugging impatiently at his shirt and he laughed quietly, his hands coming to stall her fumblings and take over. Unable to look away from him even for a moment, their gazes locked as they slipped buttons from loops, shucked clothes over heads, casting them aside, until they faced each other, naked and wanting.

She might have been self-conscious if she hadn't been able to clearly read his desire for her in the red flush slashed across his cheekbones, the glittering in his gaze, the twitch in his fingers hanging at his sides as if restrained from reaching for what they wanted: *her*.

The power she felt in that moment, the power that he had given her, was near euphoric. The vulnerability he showed as he revealed his want for her shifted something in her heart that she forced aside for the moment. Because his desire reignited hers and she couldn't wait any longer.

They came together in the middle, a tangle of limbs and sighs and kisses and touches. Sensation skated across her skin, her heart beating loud and strong, and wanting more.

'Gabi, wait—'

'No,' she returned. She'd waited long enough. He couldn't make her wait any longer!

'Gabi…' He drew her name out in the air between them like a prayer, and only then did she reluctantly pull back from her exploration of his chest.

'Protection,' he whispered regretfully, and she realised that he probably didn't have any. They'd had no need of it before.

She bit her lip. 'I'm on the contraceptive pill. To regulate my periods after…' She trailed off, stupidly embarrassed despite the intimacy they were about to share. 'I was tested when I was pregnant, and everything came back negative, obviously,' she whispered, wanting the world to swallow her up.

His thumb lifted her chin, slowly raising her gaze to his. 'I've not been with anyone since you,' he confessed, her heart soaring shamelessly at his words. 'And we are about to share our bodies,' he whispered gently, 'which means that there is nothing you can tell me about yours that I would not want to hear.'

'Like cracked nipples,' she whispered to herself, remembering from before, and Nate threw his head back and laughed. She was so shocked by the sound it took her a moment before slapping him on the arm and shushing him, biting back the laughter that had sprung so beautifully between them.

This was what she'd remembered from their night together. This was what they had shared. Why was it that laughter had somehow brought them so much closer than passion? Why was it that which had forged such a deep connection? She had been devastated when it had been lost, broken apart by savage misunderstandings.

Nate collapsed beside her on the bed, unaware of

the lump forming in her throat. One that she ruthlessly pushed aside as she leant back beside him, trying not to read too much into the way he pulled her against his side, the press of his erection still delicious to her.

She wanted to bury her head in the space between the mattress and his chest, to burrow down and hide, not her embarrassment—because he'd been right, they were about to share their bodies and there shouldn't be any. But to hide her love for him. Because she knew without a doubt that it would scare him away.

Just like it had scared so many other people in her life.

'Hey,' he said, pulling her face up to him, delighted as he placed a kiss against her lips. 'Where did you go?'

'Well, I got a little bored of waiting, so—'

Her words ended in a scream as his arms swept around her, pulling her to him, and he rolled her beneath him in one swift move, pinning her wrists beside her head.

'You're not going anywhere. I'm not letting you out of my sight ever again.'

Was it real? Could he really feel like that?

He kissed the column of her throat, his teeth gently nipping at her skin, sending shivers of pleasure across her chest and shoulders. Kisses turned to touches, turned to explorations and turned to sighs and moans of pleasure as his hands slipped between her legs and played with her some more.

Throbbing and wanton, she pulled him in for another drugging kiss, thrilled by the press and possession of his tongue in her mouth, the invasion only a suggestion of what he was capable of. And then finally, *finally*, he lay between her legs and guided himself into her, slowly, carefully, but so fully that she realised in a single breath what she'd been missing since she'd fled that hotel room.

The other half of herself.

Nate held himself deep within the heaven that was his wife—his *wife*—for as long as possible. Even when every instinct within him roared for more, he stayed there, making sure that Gabi acclimatised to the intrusion of him so deep within her.

He'd known she was a virgin before they had sex the first time and had done everything in his power to make that as pleasurable an experience for her as possible, but that had been more than two years ago. His only thought was for her—her comfort, her pleasure. His own release could wait.

But surrounded by the gentle grip of her muscles, skin to skin, his mind was a kaleidoscope of images of what he'd missed. Gabi round with their children, the flush of blooming health on her cheeks, all those firsts and all those joys…

She leaned to press a kiss against his forearm, anchoring him back in the present, and when he flexed his hips just slightly she threw back her head in bliss and all he wanted was more. She tucked her pelvis and gasped as he slid in just that little bit deeper, his arms beginning to shake with the pressure of restraint.

'I want it all, Nate. Please, can you give it to me?' she asked. And he cursed himself for making her beg.

He nuzzled the sensitive spot behind her ear and

whispered, 'Anything you wish,' biting his teeth together before he could add, *my love.*

Urged on by her, each thrust took them to places he'd thought impossible to reach. He lost seconds, minutes, hours in the sounds of her gasps and pleasure, the racing of his heart tied to each slap of his body against hers, the slick and slide of their need so utterly erotic that he had never been so hard, half scared that he might remain there for ever in a near excruciating pleasure pain pinnacle, unable to cross the threshold of his orgasm.

Again and again, he forced them to the brink and back, an exquisite form of torture, desperate to make this last, desperate to make this perfect, desperate for her to feel him in her for hours, even days to come.

Pleas in a heady mix of Spanish and English filled the room, his name in a husky voice speaking of how much she had cried her need that night. Her fingers gripped him where she could, holding on or urging on, it didn't seem to matter. They were both shaking with the sheer force of holding back an orgasm that started deep within Gabi but ended with him.

They came together, pulsing and breaking in time to a rhythm that had been set nearly two and a half years ago, Nate inhaling as Gabi exhaled, creating an internal tide where she was the moon and he was the sea, destined to wash back and forth against a shore for ever, while a star-studded eternity looked on.

He pulled her close to him and rolled onto his back, unable and unwilling to break the connection between them just yet. His last thought before he closed his eyes was that she fit perfectly against him, as if she had been made for it.

* * *

Shocking pain tore through his head as he jerked awake, drenched in a cold sweat, heartbeat racing and body locked in tension so severe that he was paralysed. Forcing his reeling mind to focus, he could just make out Gabi's sleeping form on the other side of the bed. Thank God he hadn't woken her.

He sucked air in through his nose and waited for his muscles to relax enough to move, purposely trying to release each one consciously, despite knowing that no amount of willpower would work until the sleep paralysis passed from his body. Each second felt like its own infinity, each one showing him a new fresh hell of his own fears.

Something happening to his children, to Gabi, to Hope. The faces of his family, new and old, passed before him as if in some macabre reenactment of the old Dickens book, each seemingly warning of what had or could come to pass.

Fear spiralled and unwound, reforming into a new reel and starting all over again. Nausea gripped his stomach on the final fear…of two children mourning the death of their parents…and he lurched out of bed and was nearly sick.

He made it to the en suite bathroom without waking Gabi and he splashed cold water across his face, even while every single muscle in his body protested the pain and ache of the tension that had turned them into stone. His pulse raced, his breathing erratic, but he knew he had to calm down, he had to control his body. He had to.

He gave up using his hands and put his lips to the tap,

sucking in mouthfuls of water to lose the acrid bite of nausea. He sank onto the floor beside the shower, the hard tiles cool but a blessed relief from the burning that had overtaken his body.

He wiped his mouth with the back of his hand, staring at nothing while his mind hurtled at a hundred miles an hour. The headache, the tension… He knew the odds of a recurrence of the cerebral aneurism were low, less even than a single percent, especially after the type of treatment he'd received. But they weren't non-existent.

Eventually, he hauled himself off the floor and peered back into the bedroom, where Gabi was still sleeping. A fist seemed to squeeze his aching gut, seeing how delicate she was, how wronged she'd been and how much better she deserved.

He closed his eyes and counted to ten. Sucking in a lungful of air, he turned on the shower, thankful that it was super quiet, quickly washed off the horror and fear from his body and, after drying himself thoroughly, he crept back into bed.

As if nothing had happened.

Gabi woke in an instant, her eyes springing open as her consciousness broke through the barrier of sleep. Bed. She was in her bed. A delicious ache threaded through muscles and skin that felt sensitised and warm but shivery too, even now, just from the memory of last night.

She pinned her bottom lip with her teeth, a lip that was slightly swollen and a chin that was just a little pinker, she'd imagine, than it had been yesterday. *Gracias a Dios!* Nate didn't have stubble. She was about to get up when an arm sneaked around her waist, pulling her back against a hot, hard body.

'Where do you think you're going?' Nate demanded in a voice thick with gravel and desire.

Gabi squeaked in surprise. It hadn't even crossed her mind that he would still be here, half convinced she remembered waking last night and finding the bed empty, being disappointed that he'd not stayed with her. But it must have been a dream, a projection, because Nate was most definitely still here in bed with her. His skin was warm and smooth against hers, surrounding her in an almost blissful heat that she never wanted to leave.

She burrowed back against him, but when he shifted, sliding his knee between her legs, she felt the ridge of his arousal against her and unconsciously arched into him. His hands began to wander, smoothing over sensitive skin, her hips, between her legs, her breasts, all beginning to flush beneath his attention.

'Good morning,' he whispered in her ear, bringing a smile to her lips.

'Morning,' she whispered back, the word turning into a moan as he delved between her legs, seemingly very interested in the damp heat he found there.

'We shouldn't—'

'You have somewhere else you'd rather be?' he asked, half laughing, not stopping his exploration even a little.

'No, it's just that I should… I should wake the twins,' she said as her body shuddered beneath his touch. Her nipples hardened and her skin ached for more.

'Actually, Jorge and I are going to look after the twins today.'

'What about me?' she said around a gasp as Nate managed to hold onto the conversation as if he were not playing a sensually torturous game with her.

'You are going to spend some time with your sketch-pad. Whether that's in your office or out in town, or at a coffee shop… Anywhere you need to be, our driver will take you.'

His hands fell back as she pulled away to turn and look at him. 'But—'

'No buts. We're starting again. And this time you are going to make sure that you are as much of a prior-ity as they are.'

'And I'm doing this with a sketchpad?' she asked, confused.

'Yes, Hope wants to see six designs by the end of the month.'

'What?' she demanded, her body going stock still in shock.

'Yes, didn't I tell you?' Nate asked innocently, as if he didn't know.

She leaned across the bed, grabbed a pillow and tried to hit him with it. 'No, you didn't tell me!' Her task was made harder because he was behind her and using her own body as a shield, while laughing.

'Well, now I have. But right now I don't want to talk about my sister, Gabi,' he said, his tone suddenly seri-ous and utterly sexy. He was looking at her as if he were starving and it wasn't for breakfast.

'The kids…' she tried again meekly, knowing that she wanted nothing more than for Nate to feast on her.

'The kids are still asleep and will be for at least another thirty minutes.'

'Thirty minutes?' she queried.

'I can do a lot in thirty minutes,' he replied, cocky and confident in a way that made her want to know exactly what he meant.

'Show me,' she commanded.

And he did.

Twice.

CHAPTER ELEVEN

GABI HAD RUN the gamut of emotions in the last month and it had left her exhausted…but so fulfilled. At first, she'd been utterly delighted with the idea of time to spend on her designs, and although she'd not actually been able to spend Antonio's first day home with her sketchpad as Nate had suggested—unwilling and unready to be away from her son just then—she did slowly begin to take time for herself. An hour here and there turned into two, then three.

But the first time she'd taken herself away to spend a full day on her work had been an utter disaster. Nothing had come. Well, nothing but self-doubt and negative thinking. She'd stared at a blank page, thinking, *Six designs... six designs for Harcourts' CEO.* It didn't matter that Hope was her sister-in-law, she just couldn't channel *anything* onto the page. In her mind, instead of the creative muse, she heard her mother's voice.

'It's sweet that you try, mija. It means so much that you want to be involved in my business…'

'It's pretty, but it's just not good. *I'm sorry.'*

'I would make it in a heartbeat, Gabriella, but who would buy it?'

Each one had cut a fresh wound over old scars and by the time she'd returned home she'd been a wreck. Nothing was worth feeling like this, not even her designs. She'd wanted to burn her sketchpad and had been ready to tear out the few new ideas she had forced out onto the page.

Nate had come to find her, watched her while she paced back and forth in the study.

'This was silly. A waste of time,' Gabi said, her thoughts still a jumble and feeling embarrassed. Why had she thought that she could even do it? Let alone produce six designs. 'I should be here with the kids,' she said and she meant it too. It had been a transition as gentle as it could have been, but she missed them when she wasn't with them, worried that they were missing her, worried that they saw it as a rejection. A rejection she knew so well.

She sat on the chair and put her head in her hands, pressing at her temples. It was all so much—too much of a mess. She should just stop. They'd give Jorge a good reference, he'd find more work in no time and she could come back to looking after the twins.

Nate leaned against the large drawing desk he'd fitted her office with.

'What happened?' he asked carefully.

'Nothing happened. Nothing at all!' she groaned, embarrassed to admit it. 'Look, I know you put a word in for me with Hope, but I think it was a mistake.'

'I didn't,' Nate said quietly. 'Hope has always been the one with an eye for fashion. I've always had a talent for numbers,' he said, shrugging. 'She came to me. But I'll let her know you're not interested.'

Gabi looked up. 'I *am* interested. Oh, God, I want it so much, Nate. But I'm just not good enough,' she admitted helplessly. 'I couldn't draw a thing today. Not a single thing. And the designs I do have are mediocre at best, bland. Just bad. Pathetic,' she ended on a whisper, knowing that the disdain in her voice was her mother's, not her own.

Nate squinted at her as if he could tell, as if he knew. 'Who told you that?'

'I don't need anyone to tell me that,' she said.

'Oh. So you told yourself that?'

She glared up at him, resenting what he was getting at. 'I don't want to do this right now,' she said, getting up, but he caught her by the wrist and gently pulled her in front of him.

'Who told you that?'

She shook her head, but still said, 'My mother.'

He nodded sadly, pushing a long, lazy twist of hair back from where it had hung over her shoulder. 'I'm sorry that she said those things to you. She shouldn't have.'

Gabi bit her lip, feeling hot, heavy tears press at the corners of her eyes. Nate cupped her jaw, his thumb smoothing over her cheekbone, and she couldn't help but lean against the warmth and comfort he was offering her.

'Can I say something that might hurt, but also might help?' he asked.

She bit her lip, unsure whether she could take any more hurt right now, but eventually she nodded.

'Your mother wasn't there today. She hasn't seen those designs. She didn't say those things to you. Those words were echoes of the fear you feel. That fear is stopping you from *enjoying* your creativity. If these designs go to my sister, great. If they don't, who cares?' he said with a shrug. 'But stifling your creativity, stopping yourself from doing something you *enjoy*? That's not okay. And you know that's not okay, because you would never allow your children to give in to their fears like this.'

Nate was right. She hated that he was, because it meant she had said those things to herself. But realising that it was her and not her mother meant that she could control what she said to herself, that maybe she could accept and move through that fear...

And *that* gave her power.

A power she used, bit by bit, the next day and the days that followed. She kept going back to her designs—they weren't always perfect, but she was persistent. And eventually she delved deeper and deeper into that inner core of creativity. She created designs *she* wanted to see and feel against her skin, textures and colours that were sometimes just functional, for a mother or a working woman, and other times daring, for a woman embracing and enjoying her sensuality.

Because if Nate had been determined for her to rediscover her creativity, then he was ruthless in his pursuit of her sensuality. Her nights were filled with passionate exploration and wondrous discovery of her own pleasure, and his. She could tell, she could sense it, that he had never been as connected to anyone as he was to her. Otherwise, there was no way that she could feel what she felt for him, surely.

Which was why she knew that there were times when he withdrew from her. An hour in an afternoon, two on the occasional morning. Sometimes she would wake to find the bed empty and he'd explain it away with an urgent meeting in a different time zone. There would always be an excuse. But she couldn't help feeling that, even as they drew closer, they were falling further apart. And even if she tried to tell herself it was nothing like Renata, that he wasn't manipulating her like her mother had, she couldn't help but feel that he was keeping something from her, and that was the one thing that could break them apart.

'Okay, Nathanial. You're booked in on the twelfth, the day after tomorrow, at three p.m.,' Dr Brunner confirmed.

'Okay,' was all Nate could say, finally having caved and called his neurologist.

'And is Gabi going to be joining us?'

Nate swallowed. 'Not this time.'

'Does she know?' Dr Brunner asked, as always more perceptive than anyone would credit. 'Have you told her?' he asked again in the midst of Nate's silence.

'I don't want to worry her,' Nate said, irritated with his own show of defensiveness.

'Nathanial, her support is a vital part of your recovery.'

'You call this a recovery, Doc?' Nate bit out through

clenched teeth. In the last month, his headaches had become worse. His palpitations would come on at any time during the day. There was no rhyme or reason to the episodes and it had become near impossible to keep them from Gabi.

'We don't know what this is, it could be nothing to do with your medical history. That is why you should have her support.'

Nate felt the censure in the doctor's words, but Nate knew what he was doing. Gabi was just beginning to find her feet again after the confidence wobble at the beginning of the month. Nate trusted his sister's judgement implicitly and even if Hope hadn't insisted that Gabi's designs were excellent he'd have encouraged Gabi to follow her desires because, honestly, it seemed that absolutely no one had until now.

She deserved the time she now carved out for herself, rather than utterly sacrificing her own wants and needs for her children or, worse, him. Which was why he didn't want to worry her. He had absolutely no doubt that she'd drop everything for him and he didn't want that.

He was more than capable of handling his episodes himself. He would have to make some decisions when the test results came back, he knew that. And he would. But, until then, he just wanted to enjoy this. One last day before he left for Switzerland.

He came to stand on the threshold of the patio. He looked out across the mountain range in the distance to where it fell into the sea. It was so very different from the sleek London skyline that could be seen from his apartment in Mayfair. In just months, his entire life had changed and, God, he was thankful for it.

He looked to where Gabi, in a turquoise and fuchsia striped swimsuit that showed off every single beautiful curve of her body, tried to smooth sunscreen over wriggling little bodies desperate to get into the pool. Ana's laughter filled the air as Antonio screamed just before a splash of water so great that it slapped against the hot tiles surrounding the pool. Clapping hands, truncated Spanish, giggles and the heat of the sun surrounded him as he closed his eyes.

Nate could have laughed. Until Gabi, his life had been entirely numbers and boardrooms, grey suits, white shirts and pleasures that he'd thought enough. But he'd had no idea. Gabi had brought a world of colour, emotion and feeling to him and what would he give her in return?

He clenched his jaw and the images and fears crashed through him, as if clouds had passed over the sun. The pain, the agony, of standing by his parents' grave, Hope's hand in his, beside a grandfather who had refused to permit even a single tear. A fist punched a hole in his gut as the past became his children's future and his heartbeat pounded painfully in his chest.

In his mind, it wasn't *him* that suffered in silence, but Antonio and Ana. It wasn't him who was cut from the gentle, loving home his parents had created and sent away to share a room with six other boys, and subjected daily to either the bullying of older children or the tight-lipped meanness of teachers, but his children. *They* were the ones who forced their hurts and hopes and love behind a stony façade because they were a vulnerability that could be exploited. *They* were the ones who learned that no one would come for them, that they had to do it alone, that they had to do everything alone.

A savage pain cut through his heart, so powerful he nearly gasped.

'Estás bien?' he heard Gabi ask through the rushing of blood in his ears. Forcing a smile to his face, he nodded and waved her off, slowly turning back into the house before making his way to the bathroom, where he closed the door and collapsed. The sooner he got to Switzerland the better.

Gabi checked her watch again, hating herself for it. Nate wasn't just a few hours late—he was a day late. A whole day. She'd left messages for him on his mobile, email. She'd even called his assistant, who had repeatedly assured her that he was passing on his messages. But she hadn't heard from him since he had left for his business meeting in London two days ago.

She was scared. Scared because he hadn't done this before. Scared because it made her question how well she knew him. Scared because it reminded her that she had been here before with him, nearly two and a half years ago now. Scared because she couldn't stop the avalanche of old fears of rejection and abandonment from crashing down over her head.

Gabi paced the room, unable to let out the growl of frustration coursing through her body. Pinpricks of fear and doubt covered her skin in a thousand cuts, and her body heat fluctuated between cold sweats and hot flushes. She couldn't do this again. She couldn't live like this—with another person who hid things from her, kept their feelings under a mask. She needed honesty, she needed truth. And she knew that Nate wasn't being truthful with her. But it was more than that. It was the twins.

That morning, trying to put the children down for their nap had been awful. Ana had refused to sleep without seeing Nate. She'd been utterly inconsolable. 'Where's Papá?' she'd asked again and again. 'I want Papá.' Nothing Gabi had done, or could have done, had stopped her tears. Cheeks painfully red from crying, dark brown eyes red-rimmed, hot and desolate, Gabi had only been able to rock her back and forth as Ana cried herself to sleep, wanting her father.

Gabi knew that she would never forget that moment. It had struck too close to home for her, for her own inner child, who had felt exactly that same pull, that same need. The need for a parent, for the comfort that only a parent could provide, only to discover that they would never come.

Gabi's breath sobbed in her chest as she came to a halt in front of the French windows of the villa. She'd barely survived the absence of her father and the absolute hysteria of growing up with someone who couldn't see beyond their own needs. And somehow, in one single moment, Nate had come to embody both things.

She couldn't do it. She couldn't do this to her children. She'd made him *promise* to be here. *Promise* to tell her what was going on. And he had failed that promise. Her heart was shattering at a painfully slow pace. It was as if she could feel each tiny piece breaking off as every second passed and he still wasn't here. She loved him. She had given herself to him. She had shared her children with him and he was gone.

A small part of her wondered whether this was too much. All she was feeling…was it too much, too soon? She needed space, time. She needed to hear what he had to say. But too many years of trauma and self-doubt crashed over her like a wave she struggled to surf. She was drowning in past hurts and gasping for breath, for a lifeline when there was none.

Her mobile rang, cutting into her thoughts, and she swung between relief and fear as she looked at the name. It was Hope.

'*Sí*,' she answered, forgetting her English for a moment.

'Oh, Gabi, isn't it wonderful news?'

Gabi's mind crashed to a halt, Hope's words both confusing and unexpected. But, before she could question her, Hope pressed on. 'It must be such a relief. I mean, I know the doctors have always said that the recovery would be up and down, but honestly! This time I could actually have cried. An all-clear. It's just fantastic.'

'Yes,' Gabi replied, forcing the words out through numb lips. 'It is.'

'I'm so glad I caught him, he'd just turned his phone back on after flying back from Switzerland, so he should be with you soon. I just wanted to maybe add to the celebrations a little—'

Gabi was aware that she was making non-committal noises, but her mind was racing as quickly as her heart.

'Because I've looked over the designs, Gabi, and they're marvellous!'

'Thank you,' she said woodenly, not really sure what Hope was talking about.

'Look, obviously now is not the time, but I wanted to let you know as soon as I could, and I want you to think about where you want to go from here. I'll call in a few days to set up some proper, official time to talk, but in the meantime, just know I love them and I want more! Okay? Anyway, love you, bye.'

Gabi stood in the centre of the living room, the phone hanging loosely in her hand, trying to process what she'd just heard.

Nate hadn't been in London? He'd been in Switzerland? The doctors had given him the all-clear? So he'd been worried about his health and not telling her? He'd kept that from her and lied about where he'd been?

A white-hot blade cut through all the hurt and pain she'd felt before Hope's call. All the doubt, the questions, the agony...the love. All of it. Cut through, clean, and now she felt nothing. Absolutely nothing.

In minutes she'd decided what to do. In less than half an hour the twins, sleeping through the entire thing, were on their way with Jorge to her brother and sister-in-law's and by the time Nate walked through the front door she'd packed everything that he'd need for the immediate future. If he didn't retrieve the rest of his belongings by the end of the week, she'd burn them.

That was how cold her fury was.

In the past it was hot, hurt, devastated. But now she was older, now she had learned, *now* it was about ensuring that her children were treated better than she had been. And that made her focus as finely edged as any sword. Sharp, focused and determined.

Nate walked through the door, exhausted after an intense seventy-two hours. He'd barely had time to eat, let alone sleep or even make the call to Gabi that he'd known he should have. But what he wanted to say, he wanted to do in person. The last three days had changed everything for him and all he wanted to do was hold Gabi, kiss his children and...

As he walked into the living room he caught sight of Gabi, standing in the middle of the room, looking out through the open French windows.

'Gabi? Is everything okay?' he asked, a sudden rush of adrenaline sparking through already shorted circuits around his body.

She turned to look at him and all he could think was hollow. She looked hollow. Empty.

'What happened?' he demanded, rushing towards her, only stopping when she put up a hand between them.

She looked at him blankly for another second and then something strange came into her eyes.

She shrugged. 'Happened? Nothing happened, I don't think. Obviously, you would tell me if something had, no?'

Unease unwound like a thread from a spool, tying itself into knots and loops.

'No, I—'

'Nothing?' she asked. 'Nothing comes to mind?' she

asked, her lips pursed, colour gone from her cheeks.
'Okay,' she said with a shrug, twisting her fingers together.

No. Not her fingers. Her wedding ring.

Dread pooled in his gut.

'Gabi—'

'My name is Gabriella. To you. Now—' she nodded
as if to herself '—now it is Gabriella,' she confirmed
firmly, twisting the ring from her finger and putting it
down on the table.

She looked up at him, meeting his gaze, steady, but
cold. And, no matter what had passed between them,
Gabi had never been cold.

He didn't know what to say, he didn't know what
the rules were in this situation. He didn't know where
to start, because he wanted to tell her *everything*. He
knew he'd made a mistake the moment he'd got the results from the doctors. He knew he shouldn't have kept
her in the dark.

'I'm glad you're okay,' she said woodenly. 'I *am*,' she
insisted. 'But you can go now.'

'What? Go?' he demanded, confused. Clearly, she
knew about his trip to Switzerland and he could only
imagine how terrible that must have made her feel, but—

'Yes. You can go now,' she said, slowly enunciating
the words as if English were his second language.

'Gabi, stop.'

'I didn't ask you for much before we married, but I
told you my terms. That you were present for the children until they were twenty-one and that you told me
what was going on with you.'

Colour began to leach back into her cheeks, as if

she were struggling to push back an immense anger and hurt. He could only imagine, because he knew how much he was feeling in that moment. He could feel his family slipping through his fingers. He'd spent so long trying to protect them from a pain that was in the future, he'd not realised how much damage he was causing in the present.

'Gabi, wait. I need to explain,' he said, dropping his bag on the floor and closing the distance between them. If he could explain, if he could just touch her, hold her, she'd let him.

She took a step back.

'What was it?' she demanded. 'Why did you go to see the doctors?' She glared at him, daring him to lie to her.

'I was getting migraines. Palpitations. Chest pains,' he confessed, his mind racing as quickly as his heart, hoping to see a way through this, other than the impending doom he felt himself hurtling towards. A doom entirely of his own making.

'For how long?'

He clenched his jaw, the muscles aching in protest. 'About a month.'

Gabi's hands fell to her sides and she let out the most painfully cynical laugh. 'That long?'

He wished he could deny it. He wished he'd done things differently, but he hadn't. And only now did he realise the cost.

'I asked you. Time and time again. How many lies have you told in that month? Twelve? Thirteen? No, it must be more than that. Once a day?'

Her voice was rising towards a shout and he looked to the corridor towards the children's bedroom.

'They're not here,' she explained, following his gaze. 'Jorge has taken them to Javier and Emily's.'

Anger and loss cut through him like lightning splitting a tree trunk, but he forced himself together with sheer brute strength. He inhaled slowly, knowing that she was watching his every move. But the moment he saw the sheen of tears in her eyes he decided, restraint be damned. He closed the distance between them, reaching for her arms, but she twisted from his grasp.

'Please, Gabi. I need to explain. I thought it was back. The aneurism. I thought—'

'I don't care.'

'I know that's not true,' he insisted. 'I know you care. It's the most important part of you, your heart. It's so big—'

'It's broken, Nate,' she said, interrupting him again. 'You broke it. You. Broke. It,' she repeated, each word punctuated by a sob that slashed across his heart.

The tears fell then, rolling down her cheeks, each one causing him more pain, one after the other.

'Our daughter cried herself to sleep today for you. For hours she cried for you.'

Her words twisted his heart into painful dimensions.

'So, no. There are no explanations, Nathanial. You lied. And I *knew*! I knew you were lying to me these past weeks. But we had an agreement, so I thought, no, surely he'd tell me if something was wrong. But you didn't.'

She looked up at him, as if pleading, wishing for

him to tell her that it was all a mistake. That he hadn't done it.

'You made me question myself. You made me doubt myself and you made your children cry for you. So now, you go,' she said, pulling herself together.

'No,' he said, shaking his head, panic gripping him with a tighter fist than he'd ever felt. He couldn't leave her like this. He couldn't leave, knowing he'd made her feel those things. Why wasn't she letting him explain? If he could, then she'd understand, but she wasn't letting him.

'Don't make this harder than it needs to be,' she said.

'This deserves to be hard, Gabi. It shouldn't be easy to do,' he said, realising the truth of the words as he said them. 'It should be absolutely the hardest thing ever,' he implored. 'This is our family, our children. It should take absolutely everything we have.'

'I've given everything,' she cried. 'I did. *Me*. But you? You kept it in, kept it all to yourself. Unwilling, or unable, it doesn't matter.'

'Of course it matters. But you won't let it, will you?' he said, finally catching on to what was going on, furious that nothing he could say would change things. 'Because I was never going to be good enough, was I? You were just waiting for me to fail—as a parent or a husband. And if it hadn't been this, it would have been something else, wouldn't it?' Nate demanded.

Gabi shook her head, refusing to accept what he was saying. That cool calm that she had needed to get this far was beginning to shatter. Too many emotions were breaking through while she was trying to hold onto the lifeline of control that she needed to survive this night.

'No. That's not true.'

'It is. I can't deny that I messed up, Gabi. I lied. I was scared. I thought…' He slammed his mouth shut, as if unable to bring himself to say what he'd thought might happen to him. What the migraines might have meant. 'But what you want from me? The perfection you need from me as a father? What you want from *yourself*? It is impossible. We're not perfect. We're going to make mistakes. And so are our children.'

Outrage slashed through her. 'Of course they're going to make mistakes. *They* don't have to be perfect.'

'But *we* do? *That* is the standard you are teaching your children. No matter what you say to them, it's what they will see,' he threw back at her. 'That they have to be perfect. That it's not okay to make mistakes.'

Anger and fear had her trembling from head to toe. 'The only mistake here, Nate, is you. Now, leave. Please. Right now.'

He levelled her with a look so full of hurt and anger, but she knew he saw exactly the same thing reflected in her eyes. He waited, as if hoping that she might change her mind, take back the angry, painful, bitter words, but she didn't. She couldn't. And it was only when the door slammed behind him that she collapsed to the floor, crying just like her daughter had only hours before, for the man who had broken her heart.

CHAPTER TWELVE

NATE STARED OUT across the town of Frigiliana from the hotel room's balcony, trying to pick out the villa where his wife and children were. The cost of the room had been extortionate but anything other than a hotel room spoke of a permanence he simply couldn't accept yet.

A banging sounded against the door and he half expected to see Gabi's brother, ready to tear him limb from limb, but it was worse. It was his sister.

'What the hell do you think you're doing?' Hope demanded as she barged through the door. 'I mean, I'm glad you're okay,' she continued, looking up at him with genuinely sorrowful eyes. 'I'm glad you're not going to die,' she said, reaching for his shoulder, smoothing the sleeve of his shirt, before shoving at him and saying, 'but I could kill you right now.'

Then she stalked into the living area without sparing it a glance and turned, pinning him with a look. 'Is Gabi okay? I'm so sorry. I shouldn't have called her and said…all that. But why didn't you tell her?' she demanded. 'Why didn't you tell *me*?'

'Are *you* okay?' he demanded of his sister who, even for her, was acting…

'Oh, it's the hormones,' she confessed miserably, and Nate felt like a bastard. He'd completely forgotten that his sister and Luca were going through IVF.

'Hope—'

'Oh, God, don't you start. It's fine. *I'm fine,*' she yelled over Nate's shoulder to Luca, who was coming through the door with their bags.

'Is she?' Nate demanded under his breath.

'She's fine,' Luca explained with a raised eyebrow, warning Nate not to question it.

'Look, it's great to see you, but now's really not a good time,' he said, wondering how quickly he could get them back out of the hotel as he eyed several suitcases beside Luca, who was looking around the chaos of the suite.

'Nice place you have here,' he observed wryly.

Nate closed his eyes and put his fingers to his temples in an attempt to ward off the tension headache—that he now knew was *just* a tension headache.

'It's stress,' Dr Brunner had explained. *'You've experienced a huge amount of life-altering information in—what? Two months? Less? And before that, Nate, you nearly died. These things are as serious as it gets. And if you want to live—if you truly want to live—then you're going to have to deal with the things that are holding you back.'*

'Are you even listening to me?' Hope demanded.

'No, Hope, I wasn't,' he admitted with fraying patience. He knew his sister meant well, but he hadn't intended for her to fly out to Spain when she'd caught him at a bad moment the day before and he'd admitted half of what had happened. Only half, because he couldn't even really admit it to himself just how badly he'd messed everything up.

'Come on,' Luca said, clapping him on the shoulder and walking him into the living area, casting a disdainful glance at the mess that Nate had created in just a few days. Nate tried to ignore the look Luca shared with his wife, before gesturing to the large balcony.

Hope opened the balcony door, letting both fresh air and the gentle sounds of the night into the room and, despite himself, Nate took the deepest breath he had since he'd left his home.

Gabi's home, he thought as the knife slashed his heart in two all over again.

Luca half pressed Nate into a chair and Hope sat opposite him, holding her hand out for him to take. Nate stared at it for a moment. The affection between them as siblings had always been fierce but not demonstrative. She waited and finally Nate put his hand in hers.

'Tell me. From the beginning. Tell me everything,' she demanded.

And, for the first time in Nate's entire life, he did.

Three hours later, Hope scrunched a tissue in her hands, her lip pinned beneath her teeth as if trying to stop herself from saying something Nate should probably already know himself. Coffee cups and water glasses had piled up on the table as Hope and the husband who adored her had listened to every word he'd said. Nate could see so clearly now how Luca focused on Hope and her needs, how he filled the gaping hole caused by the loss of their parents and by the emotionally stunted childhood they'd had afterwards.

Just like Gabi had for him. Just from her presence, her laughter, her awareness of him, slowly, layer upon layer, that same hole in Nate had begun to fill. The small things she had done for him to bring him into their lives, the trust she had placed in him by sharing her children with him.

The trust he had broken.

'Nate, I know that you were scared,' Hope said, holding his hand again, 'But you can't just shut down because you're scared of losing them. It's the one way to guarantee it.'

Nate frowned, disconcerted that she had so misunderstood what he'd been feeling. 'I'm not scared of losing *them*,' he said. 'Because *they* would be okay.' He shrugged. 'And that's all that matters,' he said simply. 'I'm scared of *them* losing *me*, Hope. Of them losing me and Gabi. I'm scared, terrified, absolutely bloody demented at the thought that Ana and Antonio will go through anything remotely like what happened to *us*,' he confessed helplessly, turning away from the realisation dawning in his sister's eyes.

Realisation that morphed immediately into sympathy.

Grief as fresh and raw as it had been all those years ago punched a hole in his chest. A grief for what had been, for what could be, for his children…it was too much. His hands fisted, white knuckles revealing far too much about how close he was to breaking.

'When the migraines started and I thought it was another aneurism, all I could see was us, each standing behind a coffin. I didn't even know if it was Mum or Dad,' he said, the sadness, the anger, the fear choking him. 'I can't… What if I did that to them? To Ana and Antonio. What if they—'

He couldn't finish. His words got stuck around grief and pain and loss and he couldn't speak for trying to keep back the tears he'd never been allowed to cry.

Hope's tears were falling and he was almost envious of her ability to shed them so freely.

'Okay,' she said, slowly gathering herself. 'Okay. If something happened—*if*, then they have something we didn't, Nate.'

He looked up, wondering what on earth she was talking about.

'They have a family who love them and would do anything for them. They have me and Luca. And they have Javier and Emily. They have cousins, and while they might not have grandparents—or a reasonable version of one—there is an army of love around them and people willing to care and protect them for the rest of their lives. You and Gabi, you have given that to them. They will never be alone. They will never be cold. They will never be afraid of expressing their feelings. They will never be afraid to experiment, to learn, and they will never be afraid to love. Because *that* is the family you and Gabi are creating for them.'

'Not that they're going to lose you for a very, *very* long time,' she was quick to go on. 'Did you say any of this to Gabi?' Hope asked gently.

'I couldn't. She wouldn't let me. I know I messed up. I know I should have told her about going to Switzerland, about what I was feeling, *fearing*, but I needed to know first. I needed to know so I could manage it.'

'You can't keep that to yourself, Nate, not after everything she's been through with her parents.'

'I know that…now,' he confessed, hating that his own fear had damaged so much, not only his past but his present and maybe even his future.

'So, what are you going to do about it?' Hope half demanded, as if it were a call to arms.

Nate clenched his jaw. He knew what he wanted to do and knew what he *needed* to do. He had given her space, hoping that they might find their way back to each other. But throughout Gabi's life she had been let down, time and time again. No one had fought for her in the way that she deserved, no one had sacrificed anything for her.

So now it was time to prove just how much he loved her. In front of the world, if he had to.

'Now, I'm going to get her back.'

Gabi gently rocked Ana in her arms, trying to get her to sleep. Antonio was inconsolable, he wore his heart on his sleeve, in his tears, and in his words. But it was Ana she worried about. She'd been much quieter since Nate had left and Gabi would catch her looking for him when she thought Gabi wasn't watching.

It broke her heart every time.

For the hundredth time that day, Gabi wiped at her own tears. She honestly didn't remember crying this much before and for some reason she couldn't stop. She'd thought she'd been doing the right thing when she'd forced Nate away. She'd thought she'd been protecting herself and safeguarding her children against a parent who lied, shut down, who refused to share himself emotionally or truthfully...but it didn't feel right.

And it hurt so, so much.

She and her daughter exhaled a slow breath of air at the same time and Gabi slowly walked over to the French windows, looking out, not at the starry night sky but with memories of their last argument.

'I was never going to be good enough, was I? You were just waiting for me to fail.'

As dusk fell over the mountain range in the distance, Gabi forced herself to feel through the fear and hurt she'd experienced that day. Because the one thing Nate *had* been right about was that it should be hard. It should be difficult to break their family up. Because that was what they had become, even in such a short time. So, after gently and quietly putting her daughter to bed, she went to the kitchen, poured herself a glass of white Rioja and went outside with the baby monitor and asked herself that same question.

Had she been waiting for him to fail?

Guilt and shame unfurled slowly in her breast, enough for her to know that what she'd done wasn't sitting right with her. It wasn't that she'd been waiting for him to fail, she thought, looking into the deepest part of her soul, but that she'd been waiting for him to leave. And she'd maybe thought, somewhere irrational and hurt and craven, that if she pushed him before he left himself it wouldn't hurt so much. Her throat was thick and ached with painful emotions and she reached for the glass to wash it down with a wine she couldn't taste and didn't want.

The sound of the front door opening yanked on her heart as she thought for just a second that Nate had come back. She turned, and nearly burst into tears to see Javier and Emily with her child wrapped tightly against her chest.

'Oh, sweetheart,' Emily said, coming straight out to the patio and bending awkwardly to wrap her arms around Gabi's neck. 'It will be okay.' Emily hushed and shushed, like she would have done for her own sleeping child, who was utterly oblivious to her aunt's turmoil.

Giving up the fight, Gabi let the tears fall again, her eyes hot and heavy. 'I'm so sorry,' she said, and couldn't help saying it over and over again.

'You don't have anything to apologise for, Gabi,' her brother insisted, and even through her own misery she could hear the clear upset in his own voice.

'What is it that you think you have done that is so terrible?' Emily asked gently, sitting down slowly in the chair beside her, mindful of her sleeping child.

Gabi searched for the words. 'I kicked him out.'

'Ha,' Javier barked a quiet laugh. 'I'd like to have seen that.'

Emily slapped her husband on the arm.

'No, seriously,' Javier replied, dismissing her concern with a wave of his hand. 'I'm sure his ego could do with a little stepping on every now and then.'

'No,' Gabi insisted, shaking her head. 'I said terrible things.'

'Did he deserve them?' Emily asked.

'Well, yes…maybe?' Gabi said.

'What did he do?' Javier growled.

'He lied to me. He…he thought he might be sick and he didn't tell me.'

'He was secretive?' Emily asked, while her husband was surprisingly quiet and shamefaced.

'*Sí.*'

'And it hurt you?'

'*Sí,*' Gabi replied.

'Well, then he deserved it,' Emily proclaimed. 'Did he say *why* he kept it from you?' she asked.

Gabi looked down at her hands, twisting in her lap. 'I didn't give him a chance.'

'Because?' her brother asked, even though she could see that he already knew the answer.

'Because I was afraid that he'd talk his way out of it.'

'Like Renata,' he concluded, looking down at the table, the muscle at his jaw pulsing as he clenched his teeth.

Gabi nodded, biting her lip. Her head hurt, her eyes were sore and her heart ached as if it would never not ache again, and she just couldn't understand what her sister-in-law was talking about.

'Our mother,' Javier started slowly, 'was no mother at all,' he said, the anger burning in his eyes strong enough to last for years. 'I know how much it means for you to have the truth, to know what is going on around you, to understand the reality of it,' he said, his words working into Gabi's heart. 'But Renata's lies were ones of pure selfishness. Might it have been that Nathanial was trying to protect you?'

'You're defending him?' Gabi asked, surprised.

Javier shook his head. 'But…sometimes lies are accidental,' he said, sharing a look with his wife that Gabi couldn't quite decipher. 'It will be okay,' her brother reassured her, returning his attention to Gabi.

'How can you say that?' Gabi asked hopelessly.

'Because he loves you,' he said simply. 'Emily knows it, *his* sister knows it…*mierda*, even *I* know it. We're just all waiting for you to know it.'

Hope unfurled deep within her heart. 'But he lied,' her fears made her protest for the last time.

'Do you think he'd do it again?' Emily asked.

'I…'

Gabi realised she hadn't even considered that. She'd drawn a line right through the mistake he'd made, not even stopping to question whether he'd learn from it. Because she had been so determined to be perfect. She'd needed to be different to her mother. She'd needed her children to have a parent, *parents*, who would be… Perfect.

'We're not perfect. We're going to make mistakes…'

Her hand shook as she pressed her fingers against her lips. 'I think I've made a terrible mistake.'

'Nothing that can't be fixed in time, *mi amor*,' her brother insisted.

Buenas tardes. I'm leaving a message for Ms Gabriella Casas. Your mother's trial has resumed and we request your presence to give witness testimony on 20th September. Please call Señor Torres to confirm.

Gabi made her way up the steps of the courthouse, with Emily and Javier by her side. They'd argued about it, but Javier had finally won when he'd told her that he'd not let her face Renata alone ever again. She'd also lost the argument about bringing the children, as Jorge was visiting his mother after a particularly bad fall and Emily and Javier had insisted they would be fine.

She had wanted to call Nate for days now, but Emily had told her to leave it a bit longer. Uncomfortable with the idea of 'letting him sweat', as Emily had said, Gabi had decided that once her mother's trial was done, she would find Nate and ask him to come home.

That thought was the only thing keeping her going as she entered the courtroom with her family behind her and they were ushered into seats at the back. But when she looked up she thought she was imagining things, because there, back on the witness stand, was Nate, looking just about as handsome as she'd ever seen him.

He looked towards her, his eyes blazing with so much emotion she felt indelibly marked by it, his gaze flickering between her and the children, and her heart nearly burst from wanting to go to him.

Then he turned to look at her brother and they seemed to exchange a brief nod, and Nate turned back to the court. Gabi glared at her brother, suspicions of their collusion forming amidst her confusion, but nothing that soothed the racing of her pulse.

Nate ignored Renata Casas and now that Gabi and his family were all here he turned his attention back to the lawyer. His pulse was pounding in his chest and for the first time in ages he wasn't scared that it was some kind of medical emergency. He simply recognised it for what it was.

The love he felt for his wife and children.

'You've requested to add to your original statement, Mr Harcourt. Is that correct?'

'Yes.' He nodded.

'And why is that?'

'Since I was last here, certain things have changed and I'm aware of the plaintiff's ability to distort facts to suit her needs, so I would like the chance to set the record straight.'

The translator beside him started speaking midway through the lawyer's objection.

'This is highly unusual, your honour.'

'As is the plaintiff's miraculous recovery,' the judge sighed, deciding to overrule the objection. 'Proceed.'

'Two months ago, I was lucky enough to have Gabriella Casas agree to be my wife. She is the mother of my children and the love of my life,' he said, staring right at Gabriella. 'And I know that Renata will try to use this to make it seem that my wife and I are trying to get rid of her and steal her business. We are not. But to make sure that she cannot use any more lies against us, I want to let the court know that I have returned my shares in Casas Textiles to Gael Casas, Renata's brother. For the price of one euro.'

A gasp of shock went through the courtroom, none so loud as the cry of outrage from Renata herself, but he only had eyes for Gabi.

'In fact, it is not the only business I have shed recently. I have resigned from my position at Harcourts and sold two of the three remaining businesses that I own,' Nate explained into the small microphone on the desk.

'Is there a reason for this?' the lawyer asked.

'Yes. Two and a half years ago, I had a cerebral aneurism that ruptured, leading me to require surgery and intense rehabilitation.'

Another gasp went through the spectators and he saw the shock and surprise streak across Gabi's expressive features and he willed her to understand.

'Why are you telling us this?'

'Because Renata Casas uses lies and secrets against people and I no longer want to live with such things in my life. My wife showed me that I don't *need* to. She is the strongest, truest person I know and I don't deserve her,' he admitted, throwing himself wide open. 'Despite the damage done by Renata Casas, she is the most loving, caring mother, fiercer than any lioness, and the most incredible wife any man could ever ask for,' he said, hoping that she was hearing him, truly hearing him. 'And she will not be giving evidence here today, will she, Ms Casas?'

Nate glared at a furious Renata. Red-cheeked, bitter-eyed, teeth gritted, she slowly nodded.

'For the record, Ms Casas?' the judge demanded.

'No. She does not. I am changing my plea to guilty and…throwing myself on the court's mercy.'

Each word seemed to get stuck in her throat, but Nate didn't care. Their agreement had stipulated the specific wording she would use in court, and Nate knew without a doubt that this would hurt her more than any incarceration or financial punishment.

Yes, he had paid Renata a considerable amount of money, but his lawyers had drawn up an airtight agreement that would ensure Renata never darkened her daughter's door, or those of her grandchildren, ever again, for any reason.

By this point the courtroom was in uproar. Journalists' cameras were flashing away, the judge was yelling, Renata was staring daggers at him and he didn't care. He swept down from the stand, his eyes, his entire focus and being were only on Gabi.

He found her despite the chaos, cutting through the throng of people who had risen up to try to catch a glimpse of a cowed Renata Casas. He reached for Gabi as she came to him and the sense of relief poured over the wounds from the past weeks and years.

'I'm sorry,' he said the moment his hands were on hers. 'I didn't say that before. And it should have been the first thing out of my mouth. I am so truly sorry,' he repeated, feeling the rent in his heart that had opened not just that day, but many, many years before. His heart broke anew when he saw a tear fall down her cheek. 'I was scared,' he admitted. 'Terrified. The migraines to me meant that my aneurism was back and I couldn't see past the future I was giving Ana and Antonio. A future full of grief and devastation.'

Gabi's eyes became full of pity and sorrow and she opened her mouth as if to say something, but couldn't, and he was thankful. Because he wasn't finished.

'I was so damaged by the loss of my parents and the

years that followed, I couldn't see past my own pain. I couldn't see what withholding that from you would do to you,' he said as he came to within barely a foot from where she stood, her body heat reaching him. 'This is not an excuse,' he said, wanting so much to reach for her. 'But I want you to know that I understand that my pain made me selfish and I will never forgive myself for hurting you the way that I did.'

Her gaze became one of longing, sadness, but also something that gave him the hope he desperately needed at that point.

'You should *never* have had to question either yourself or my feelings for you, my *love* for you. And if you give me a chance, you never will again. I know I will make mistakes. This is new and strange and talking about my feelings is awkward and deeply uncomfortable, but I want to do it for you. I want to do it for us. I want to do it for our children. Because I don't want them to become what I was… What I was before I met you.'

He broke off, searching her gaze.

'I love you,' he said. 'And I want to say it again already. I want to tell you over and over and over again. I want to say those words for the rest of my life,' he admitted, feeling the sheen of tears that he'd never had the courage to shed…until now.

Gabi startled, realising the strength of his feelings, reaching up to wipe the single tear that had escaped from Nate's eye.

'Oh, Nate, it's me that's sorry. From the moment you left, I knew I was wrong.'

'You weren't,' Nate insisted, and she smiled, wondering at the two of them arguing over such a thing.

Love swelled so much in her heart she thought it would burst but, to her astonishment, it simply grew, the muscles around it becoming bigger, stretching further to make space for all the love that she felt for Nate, for her family.

'I should have let you explain. But I was scared too. I was scared to trust in the love I felt for you and the love I felt from you,' she admitted. 'And I thought that it was easier to push you away than take the risk you might leave like my father, or not even love me, like my mother.'

'I will never let you question such a thing ever again,' he vowed, and she believed him.

'But you told them, you told the *world*, about your aneurism,' she said, shocked.

'I have no need for secrets any more,' he insisted. 'My only weakness, my only vulnerability, is you and our children,' he swore.

'And your businesses?' she asked, as if he were utterly out of his mind. 'Are you sure?'

'Absolutely. Because I know what I want from life. And that's you and Ana and Antonio. If that's as your husband, then…' He clenched his jaw before releasing it. 'Oh, God, I would love that more than the world. But if not, then I will be here as their father.'

Gabi suddenly realised that she'd not told him, not said the words that were tattooed on her heart from the very first moment she'd seen him.

'I love you,' she said, reaching up to pull him in to

a hungry kiss. 'I love you so much,' she said against his lips.

For just a moment they were lost in the passion that always simmered just beneath the surface between them, until someone jostled them hard and they remembered where they were. Gabi felt a pull on her dress and found Ana careening into her arms from a slightly harassed and apologetic-looking Emily.

Glancing back to see that Javier had a firm hold on Antonio, she raised her child in her arms, but Ana only had eyes for Nate.

'Papá?' she said in such a hopeful voice that Gabi nearly burst into tears all over again.

Nate reached for her, and she went to him immediately.

'Papá!' Ana cried again, her eyes beginning to fill with tears. 'Papa here,' she said to Gabi, and this time she let the tears fall down her cheeks as her daughter looked between both of her parents and clapped, happy for the first time since Nate had left.

Nate gazed at Gabi, all the love shining in his eyes for her, for their children, and she knew that they would be okay, finally beginning to understand that marriage, love, wasn't about being perfect and achieving excellence. It was about messing up and learning about each other and about themselves, and it was about loving and accepting all the parts that came in between. That there would be arguments to come and disagreements and maybe even battles, but they would survive them all if they loved each other and relied on all the support they could get.

'Papá no go,' Ana ordered. 'No go,' she said again.

'I'm not leaving,' Nate swore, there and then. 'I'm never going anywhere without you again. Without *any* of you,' he said, staring into his wife's eyes, knowing that this time when he saw the future for his family it was filled with nothing but love.

EPILOGUE

'I DON'T LIKE IT. We're completely outnumbered,' Javier complained.

'The odds are not in our favour,' Luca agreed gravely.

'But they're just girls,' Antonio replied, before the men turned on him with a 'Woah,' a 'Hold on a minute', and a 'Don't let your mother hear you talking like that!'

Nate pulled his nearly teenage son into his side by his shoulders. 'Come here, I want to show you something.' He led his son out onto the balcony of the house located just outside of Málaga.

Four years ago, the three families had come together to buy a house big enough for all of them to get together in the summertime, or over the winter school breaks. It had become Nate's second favourite place in the world, after the home he shared with his wife and children.

Beyond the balcony, Nate and Antonio could see down into the garden, to the table where the women had gathered together to form their own plan of attack.

'What do you see?' he asked his son, pride beating fiercely in his chest, not only for his wife and daughter, but his sisters—by blood and marriage—and his nieces.

Family. That was what *he* saw, but what he wanted Antonio to see was something different.

'They have a map.'

'Yes, they do. Which means that...'

'They have a plan.'

'Yes, they do,' Nate agreed.

'They're clever,' Antonio concluded. 'Sneaky. Ana will probably be the worst.'

'Or the best,' Nate countered.

'So, I should take her out first?' Antonio looked up at his father for approval.

'So you should not, ever, underestimate the women of this family, or any other woman, for that matter,' Nate chided. 'But yes, you should probably try and get Ana out of the game first,' he agreed.

Luca threw his head back and laughed.

'I don't know what you think is so funny. You probably have the most expertise here and you're being the least help!' Javier growled harmlessly.

'We all decided that it was only fair if I do what I'm told, rather than take any tactical role.'

'But Papá, if we're not supposed to underestimate women, then why can't we have Uncle Luca's help?' asked Antonio.

'He's got a point,' Nate admitted.

'No time,' Javier called as the large clock on the games room wall ticked down. 'We're a go!'

Everyone grabbed their water pistols and fanned out and for the next hour and a half the annual water fight consumed everyone's thoughts.

Well, mostly everyone's. The second Nate had seen

his wife trying to sneak past the pergola, he'd swept her up in his arms and drew her back around the side of the house. He moved the hand he'd placed over her mouth and covered her lips with his. What he'd intended to be a fun, momentary distraction turned carnal almost instantly—as it always did, the feel of his wife beneath his hands and mouth intoxicating and addictive. His feelings for her hadn't lessened over the years but increased. There were a few grey streaks in her hair, as there were in his, but it only made her look more beautiful to him.

'Nate,' she managed, slapping him on the arm as he abandoned her mouth to kiss his way down her neck, his hands wandering to her skirts, even as she slapped them away. 'PG Thirteen,' she warned, as conscious of the family that surrounded them as he was.

'Okay,' Nate grumbled in agreement. 'Above the neckline,' he groused, returning his lips to hers.

They smiled as they heard shrieks and cries coming from the kids—and even some of the adults, everyone enjoying the yearly competition that had grown innocently enough from a disagreement between Emily and Javier that had ended in a water fight much smaller than the one currently being waged.

Gabi moaned into Nate's mouth and he'd never tire of hearing the sound, the effect on him instantaneous.

'Let's go back to our room,' he said, trying to entice her away from the fun.

'Mmm… So tempting,' she said, and he knew she meant it. He could see it in her eyes. 'But you'll have to wait—we have a war to win,' she said, just before she brought up the water pistol and sprayed him in the chest.

Laughing, she spun out of his hold and ran back out into the garden with an impressive war cry, and he thought he'd never loved her more than in that moment. He'd never not be grateful for her capacity for forgiveness, knowing that he'd come so close to not having this in his life, not only once but twice, and he had absolutely no intention of pushing it to a third time.

He hung back at the corner of the estate, watching arcs of water jet through the air, creating rainbows nearly everywhere he looked. Hope and Luca had joined forces against their two children, Felicity and Bella, and on the other side of the garden Emily had just pushed Javier into the pool, much to the delight of Lily, their one and only daughter but the light and love of their lives.

But it was Gabi on whom his gaze anchored, taking on both of their children at once. Ana and Antonio combining their forces was a sight that would always bring joy and peace to their parents' hearts.

At night they would all come together around the table and share meals, drinks, stories and even sometimes songs. Javier, always with his arm around Emily's shoulders and a smile for his daughter. Luca, his girls in his arms and his heart in his eyes for Hope. This was what Gabi had brought to him. A family, full of joy and love, in ways he never would have imagined years before.

He'd never, not even once, regretted scaling back his businesses and instead, as the children had got older and gone to school and his time had become more free, he'd focused instead on the charity work he'd begun with Luca and Javier.

He'd watched in awe as Gabi had embraced her creativity and, rather than selling her designs to Harcourts, had joined with Hope and another woman, Sofia Obeid, to start a small but immensely successful fashion brand. Seeing her negotiate herself as a designer, a business owner, a mother, a sister, a friend…it had been a pleasure for him, and an important lesson for their children. One that he was watching have a direct impact on them as they grew into the young teenagers they were becoming.

And in his later years he'd be able to look back and know that he'd lived up to his promise—that his children hadn't had the same cold, isolated childhood that he and his sister had. That the love that Gabi had drawn from him had bloomed and grown into a garden that many future generations would benefit from. But nothing meant more to him than the love of his wife, his heart, his other half: Gabriella Harcourt.

* * * * *

Were you swept up in the drama of
Twin Consequences of That Night?
If so, then make sure to check out
these other fabulous Pippa Roscoe stories!

Claimed to Save His Crown
The Wife the Spaniard Never Forgot
Expecting Her Enemy's Heir
His Jet-Set Nights with the Innocent
In Bed with Her Billionaire Bodyguard

Available now!